In the Land of Happy Tears

IN THE LAND OF HAPPY TEARS

YIDDISH TALES FOR MODERN TIMES

COLLECTED AND EDITED BY
DAVID STROMBERG

DELACORTE PRESS

Visit us on the Web! GetUnderlined.com

Educators and librarians, for a variety of teaching tools, visit us at
RHTeachersLibrarians.com

Library of Congress Cataloging-in-Publication Data
Names: Stromberg, David, editor.
Title: In the land of happy tears : Yiddish tales for modern times / collected and edited by David Stromberg.
Description: First edition. | New York : Delacorte Press, [2018] |
Summary: A collection of stories from the early- and mid-20th century Yiddish literary tradition, in a variety of genres, by Eastern European writers such as Moyshe Nadir, Jacob Reisfeder, and Sonya Kantor.
Identifiers: LCCN 2018015386 (print) | LCCN 2018022073 (ebook) |
ISBN 978-1-5247-2035-3 (ebook) | ISBN 978-1-5247-2033-9 (hardback) |
ISBN 978-1-5247-2034-6 (library binding)
Subjects: LCSH: Jews—Juvenile fiction. | Children's stories, Yiddish—
Translations into English. | CYAC: Jews—Fiction. | Conduct of life—Fiction.
| Short stories. | BISAC: JUVENILE FICTION / Fairy Tales & Folklore / Anthologies. | JUVENILE FICTION / Religious / Jewish. | JUVENILE FICTION / Social Issues / Values & Virtues.
Classification: LCC PZ5 (ebook) | LCC PZ5 .I377 2018 (print) | DDC [Fic]—dc23

The text of this book is set in 11.5-point Latienne.
Interior design by Stephanie Moss

Printed in the United States of America
10 9 8 7 6 5 4 3 2 1
First Edition

For Noa and the
unique power of every soul

CONTENTS

WHAT IS YIDDISH, ANYWAY?

YIDDISH: A CULTURE OF RESILIENCE

When people think of Yiddish, what usually comes to mind is an Old World Jewish language that today is used mostly to be funny. Humor actually *is* one of the more conspicuous elements of Yiddish that have passed from old Europe into American culture. Part of the explanation is that to most American ears, Yiddish *sounds* funny. Yiddish words like *klutz, futz, putz, schmooze, schmaltz, schmuck, chutzpah, tchotchke, bupkes, glitch, schlep, nosh, kvetch, kibitz,* and *kitsch* are in English dictionaries and often find their way into jokes. Yiddish sometimes also offers ways of describing actions with a twist. It's one thing to have a talk with someone, but something else to schmooze them—even though, in the original Yiddish, *shmues* just means having a chat.

Yiddish was brought to America during the immense wave of immigration that took place from the 1880s to the 1920s, when over two million Eastern European Jews entered the United States. Many came from cities and towns where they had been peddlers, merchants, and tradespeople. Escaping persecution, they were pursuing a new start in America and settling in urban centers like New York City's Lower East Side, where many ended up leaving their trades and working in emerging industries—like the garment industry. Most of these Yiddish-speaking Jews did not have the time or means to go back to school, instead learning English on the street. And as they did, they incorporated the untranslatable parts of Yiddish into their adoptive language, creating new meanings that had not existed before. These Yiddish words were picked up by other English speakers, enabling them to describe aspects of city life that did not yet have their own expressions. Together with the beginnings of the Great Migration, when over a million African Americans moved from the rural South to urban centers and introduced language that became a dominant part of American English, the immigration of Yiddish speakers influenced the language in ways that have remained to this day. The result was an urban English inflected with Eastern European Jewish life, picking up its humor but also its gravitas—since life in the Old World, with its pogroms and poverty, drove not just the need to immigrate but also the appetite for humor.

Life in America—with its factories, sweatshops, and tenements—was not necessarily easier. But at least it offered hope for greater prosperity and social acceptance.

As Jewish immigrants integrated into modern city life, they also left behind their traditional lifestyles, making Yiddish seem like a language from the past. This shift was similar to adaptation processes in many immigrant communities. But Lower East Side Yiddish was no more a language of the past than the Chinese of Chinatown or the Italian of Little Italy.

Compared with those languages, actually, Yiddish was quite young, having begun to develop only in late medieval times. Yiddish had its roots among the Jews of southern Europe, who—speaking Old Italian and French—moved northward and settled along the major rivers of German lands. Their religious language, incorporating Hebrew and Aramaic texts, was fused with Middle High German, which they wrote out in Hebrew letters. In the Late Middle Ages, persecution and expulsion pushed Jews farther east to Slavic lands, and Yiddish began to be filled with Slavic words and grammar, while continuing to be written in the Hebrew alphabet. It soon developed into a language unlike any that had ever existed: a Semitic-Germano-Slavic tongue that traced a thousand years of Jewish life in Europe.

This history and culture were wrapped in the bundle of a unique language, alive in its people, who brought it along with them when they immigrated to America.

And just as Hebrew, German, and Slavic words had made their way into Yiddish, Yiddish words now made their way into English. This may be partly because Yiddish and English share Germanic roots. Yiddish also changes the stress patterns of words with different linguistic origins—like *schvitz* or *tchotchke* or *meshugah*—in a way that allows them to also work in English. Even the Slavic ending *-nik*, which in German or English would be *-er* (as in *swimmer*), made its way into English with a word like *Beatnik*.

As Yiddish words move into English, they take on additional meanings, but also lose parts of their original meanings, which are often slippery. In Yiddish, a *kibets* is a group or community, from which the Hebrew word *kibbutz*, or collective farm, is derived, while a *kibetser* is an interfering onlooker, someone we call in English a kibitzer. *Kibets* and *kibetser* sound similar, but their linguistic roots and Yiddish spellings are different—the first word comes from Hebrew and the second from German—which is why someone from a kibbutz can be both a kibbutznik and a kibitzer. When the great children's author-illustrator William Steig needed a name for his lovable green ogre, he harked back to the Yiddish of his Jewish immigrant roots, calling him Shrek—which in English is simply *Terrible*.

But there is more to Yiddish humor than funny-sounding words. Yiddish has a long and rich history of storytelling that goes back in print to the *Mayse Bukh* (1602), a collection of tales and legends. Many tales were told about the founder of Hasidism, Rabbi Israel ben Eliezer, better known as the Baal Shem Tov—a Hebrew phrase that can be interpreted to mean both Master of the Good Name (of God) and a kind of faith healer—turning him into a living legend, who made his way from oral tales to written collections. In the early 1800s, Rabbi Nachman of Breslov, the Baal Shem Tov's great-grandson, reinvented Yiddish storytelling through deceptively simple stories that had religious, mystical, and political themes. These tales, written down by one of his students and later circulated in printed copies, are considered the prototype for modern Yiddish storytelling. After Rabbi Nachman came three secular writers—S. Y. Abramovich, who wrote under the pen name Mendele the Book Peddler (1836-1917), I. L. Peretz (1852-1915), and S. N. Rabinovich, best known as Sholem Aleichem (1859-1916)—often called the founders of modern Yiddish literature. These authors, unlike generations before them, had left religious life, using both humor and parody to depict the transition from the old to the new—which Jews, like people of many other cultures, were facing at the time. They sometimes harnessed the rhetorical style of Talmudic argumentation but applied it to the secular world—exposing the gap between traditional and modern life, which increasingly split Jewish culture and society.

These great writers developed a modern Yiddish literary tradition, incorporating new themes and genres, including literature for younger readers. The first such story is generally considered to be Sholem Aleichem's "The Penknife" (1886), though it was originally written for adults and was only later adapted for a younger audience by the author. This approach set a tone for Yiddish literature—relating to young people as readers in their own right, worthy of the highest literary standards, with a moral compass of their own. A variety of periodicals and booklets were published in the first half of the twentieth century, full of tales portraying experiences to which younger Yiddish speakers could relate. While stories for adults exposed social conditions, sometimes in a parodic light to help readers laugh about their circumstances, tales for younger readers also aimed to pass on Old World values at a time of quickly changing realities. They sought to equip young people in Yiddish-speaking communities with tools to face circumstances that were then driving millions of Jews—whose forebears had lived in Eastern Europe for hundreds of years—to move halfway across the world in search of a better life.

Abramovich and Peretz never made it out of Europe, but in 1906 Sholem Aleichem arrived in New York City, where he was received as a living icon of Yiddish culture. But he was not as successful in America as he had hoped, and despite failing health, he returned to Europe a year later—only to flee again after the outbreak of World War I in 1914. His second stay in New York was as unsuccessful as his first, but Yiddish readers still loved his early stories. His premature death in 1916 revealed the immense significance he held for Yiddish culture, with a funeral procession estimated at well over a hundred thousand people—about a quarter of all Jews living on the Lower East Side. Reporting on the procession, the *New York Times* wrote that "extra precaution by the police prevented a repetition of what occurred at the funeral of Rabbi Jacob Joseph"—when, in 1902, a procession estimated at fifty to a hundred thousand mourners attracted anti-Jewish violence and ended in a riot. Sholem Aleichem's procession, managed by a police force of two hundred, came to a peaceful end in a show of cultural community unlike any seen before in New York City. And it reflected a change in the cultural makeup of American Jews. For the Jews of the Lower

East Side, Yiddish literature, now apparently even more than religion, was their great binding force.

Sholem Aleichem was never forgotten. And neither was the humor he brought to Yiddish speakers in America—which was translated into English as Jews developed a local identity of their own. As they became established in American society, Jewish cultural producers re-created images of the past, recasting Sholem Aleichem's stories about Tevye the dairyman—his now-beloved village character—into the musical *Fiddler on the Roof.* Some saw this as the victory of Yiddish culture in America, while others saw it as a defeat. The struggle for better social standing had created a disconnect from what life in Eastern Europe had been like. The poverty that had led to Jewish immigration, the persecution suffered by earlier generations, and the increase of anti-Semitism in the period before World War II—all these were largely eclipsed by the aim to achieve prosperity, accompanied by a romanticizing nostalgia. The grittier aspects of life in Eastern Europe were lost and, with them, some of the values and lessons that had been passed down through the generations.

Yet traces of this past survived in tales for young readers, published in booklets that were sold across Eastern Europe and America. These booklets preserved the art of Yiddish storytelling, along with and the Eastern European Jewish imagination, conveying traditional principles while taking into account the world's new realities. They were written for young readers both in the Old and New Worlds, reflecting their lives while aiming to instill in them the values that had been lost with modernity. Some of the stories portray harsh realities that are difficult to imagine, but they are authentic indications of what it meant to be a Jewish child in Eastern Europe. The stories were authored in the interwar years by women and men who spoke to young readers about a cultural environment in transition from the past to the present—with everlasting dangers that were growing to an unprecedented scale.

The morals in their stories are both noble and practical. They deal with the powers we don't always know we have, and prepare us for all kinds of circumstances—helping us think about unexpected situations and reminding us that this world, no matter how difficult or scary, is our own. The stories help us examine our behavior—and that of others—while repeatedly showing that dialogue, tolerance, and compassion are our best tools when dealing with conflict. They may not always be funny in the way we expect of Yiddish tales, but they embody the strength that Yiddish showed throughout the twentieth century.

The death blow to Yiddish culture, which was already threatened by cultural adaptation in America, came with World War II, when the Holocaust—also called the *Shoah*, or "catastrophe" in Hebrew—destroyed millions of lives and decimated most of the Yiddish-speaking communities in Europe. The Jews who were murdered have often been considered passive victims, but they were actually quite resilient, losing their lives only to the worst of modern history. Nothing could prepare them for the coming disaster, but the stories on which they grew up make tangible the culture of resilience with which they faced their destruction.

The realities that led Jews to immigrate to the United States, no less than the atrocities that annihilated most of those who remained in Europe, have become part of the collective history that makes Americans—and the English language—what they are today. But some of the powerful aspects of Yiddish storytelling have been muffled during its adaptation into American culture. The stories in this collection, which are as vital now as they were a hundred years ago, give voice to the broader spirit of Yiddish, helping young people become aware of something they are often made to forget: their own powers.

Since these powers have interconnected aspects, the stories have been grouped to highlight several core principles: *bravery, rebellion, justice,* and *wonder.* These principles have deep roots in the Eastern European Jewish tradition—in both Hasidic and non-Hasidic teachings—as found in concepts like *tikkun,* which strives to correct the wrongs of the world; in *bitul,* which reaches beyond the material world toward higher values; in *musar,* the study of Jewish ethics; and in *hitpa'alut,* wonder and awe at the great mystery of life. Together, the stories show us what it means to put these powers into effect, both in the realm of the spirit and in the world where we live.

The collection points back to a time that is closer than people think, a shared past that was almost lost but can be experienced one story at a time. Whether in the real world of the *heder* (literally "room"), where boys studied Hebrew and religion from an early age, or in fantastical worlds of kings, queens, and forest animals, where women turn from flesh to stone and back again, these tales reveal the mind-sets of their writers and readers, and the culture of resilience exemplified by Yiddish. The collection puts flesh onto the Jewish imagination of Eastern Europe—which America inherited and nearly forgot—offering a chance to experience the world in which these stories were created. In this busy era, when senseless events take up most of our daily attention, this collection gives readers a chance to dip in and out of a world that is oddly familiar—reminding them of a past that is always about to be forgotten but that always feels somehow so similar to the present.

These tales, carefully collected and translated, appear in English for the first time. Their authors, some writing while still in Europe and others after arriving in America, conveyed an impressive array of Yiddish powers that have stood the test of time. By portraying the images and values of a traditional life that was being upended, these authors created entry points into the past, not only for Jewish children of the time, but for all future readers. The world reflected in their stories is not always simple, but its manifold inhabitants are never altogether discouraged. Theirs is a land where happiness comes with tears—and where even tears are happy.

—David Stromberg, Jerusalem

BRAVERY

IN THE LAND OF HAPPY TEARS

Moyshe Nadir

Listen here, children. Do you want to hear something you've never heard before? Then sit yourselves down on this bench, like good children, and I'll tell you a story.

If you've ever studied geography, then you know that not far from Mount Hotzemklotzem lies a river called the Ampsel.

All week long, the river Ampsel spews a boiling sealing wax that makes it impossible to even get close. If you do, you instantly get sealed up—a package ready for the Angel of Souls, who stands by with an inkwell, immediately writes down an address, and sends you off to the World to Come.

But once in 666 years, when the Sabbath falls on a Wednesday, you can approach the river backward so it thinks you're actually walking away. And when you're just close enough, you throw a red onion over your shoulder and say three times:

Echepeche meche-merly.
Little river, it's still early.

This scares the river Ampsel, and it freezes with trembling waves on both sides, like the angry lips of an irate person whose mouth has opened and can't be shut. And that's when you jump off Mount Hotzemklotzem, sitting on your hands—which you hold together under yourself like a little bench—and start flying wherever you want. You fly for a day and a night, and then another day and a night, until you fly into the very middle of Shortfriday and tear it into two halves. One half runs off to the left, the second to the right, and you end up standing just where you ought to be, that is: in Tearania.

This is obviously easier said than done. Before you break into Tearania, you have to first bathe in the Goldwater of Ashm, where the Ampsel flows into the Krikrama. When you come out, you look like a golden figure on a sign—completely gold and, besides that, not moving your feet. The Goldwater of Ashm has this quality that whoever bathes in its waters starts walking with their neck. That is, your feet stand or sit in place, while your neck stretches out on its own and your head goes wherever you want it to. That's why all the inhabitants of Tearania have such long necks—except when their necks come back to them.

But the main story we want to tell you, children, is about the salt that doesn't exist there and that, if it were to exist, would possibly make it the happiest place in the world!

It's like this. The region around the Ampsel is very rich. The soil is not actually soil but rich, freshly baked bread. When you're hungry, you tear off a piece of hot soil and eat.

Or when you want meat, you don't need to spill any blood, the way we do, but what? You just unzip the hide of a cow or an ox. (Hides in this place are undone with zippers under the bellies.) You tear off whatever piece of meat you want—you just have to leave behind the end, and soon a new animal grows beneath the very same hide. And it doesn't even feel that it's a different animal.

As for rain—in Tearania, it rains wine. If you want to sleep, there are mountains made of cotton balls. Otherwise you just sneeze and geese come flying, stuffing themselves inside white pillowcases they carry in their little bills, and you sleep to your heart's content.

But there's one thing, children, they don't have in Tearania: salt!

They have everything: gold and silver, coal and oil, iron and copper, brass and tin, bread and meat, honey and almonds, icebox cakes and malted milk shakes. And in short, it's a place where you can live and laugh.

Laugh? No. I haven't told the truth. In Tearania, people cry more than they laugh. That is, they could laugh in Tearania, and why not? Such a land! Such plenty! Such soil! Such animals! But what? It's just the same thing again: salt!

Since there's no salt, parents smack their children so that their tears salt the bread. And when children refuse to cry, they get smacked even more. And if they don't want to cry straight onto the bread, they get a proper swat. After the children have cried out all their tears and salted their little lunches, the whole story starts all over again with dinner.

The mother says to the father:

"You have to cry out the bread today."

The father says to the mother:

"Me? Why me? You can cry! I feel joy in my heart today—I've had some brandy."

"Is that so?" says the mother. "You're becoming a drunk on top of it all!" And she starts to cry.

The father rushes over and slides a fresh cucumber just under her eyes.

The mother says to the father:

"Take that cucumber away, you drunkard."

The father says to the mother:

"Don't be silly. I just said that because an unsalted cucumber has no taste."

These kinds of scenes would occur in Tearania almost every day. Until one person—a wise man and watchmaker—invented a patent. Instead of smacking children or upsetting wives, people would be better off if, at every meal, they placed a lady near the table to grate horseradish, so that tears would flow from everyone and fall straight into their bowls of noodle soup—or onto their hot dumplings.

Translated by David Stromberg

AN AUTUMN TALE

Leon Elbe

Near the river there grew trees, and on the trees grew leaves.

The spring had colored the leaves green, and this is how they stayed all summer. But autumn didn't like the green of the leaves, and when it arrived, it started to paint them, some yellow and some red. And then wild winds came and tore the leaves off the trees and whipped them to the ground—and also made them dance and spin like crazy.

"Woooo," howled the wild winds, driving the leaves off the trees, "down from the trreeees. . . ."

And the leaves pleaded with the wild winds:

"Why are you taking us off the trees? We leaves make shade, and people come to rest and cool themselves off in our shade."

The wild winds kept howling:

"It's getting cold, and people don't need shade any-more. . . . They want to warm up now, not cool off. Woooo . . . down from the trreeees. . . ."

The leaves pleaded again:

"But have pity on the trees! They'll be bare and naked, without a single leaf to cover them, and what will they do in the cold?"

The wild winds howled:

"Woooo . . . Uncle Snow is coming soon and he'll cover the trees with a white blanket and they won't be cold. . . . Woooo . . . down from the trreeees. . . ."

No amount of pleading helped the leaves, and they had to come down off the trees one by one. One leaf, a yellow one, called out to another leaf, a red one:

"You know what, brother leaf? Why should we fall onto the ground and be cast off who-knows-where or get trampled by human feet or horses' hooves—or, worse still, turn into dirt and mud? Since we're near a river, let's fall into the river, where no one will trample us with their feet. The river's clean and smooth, and we'll swim along. We'll swim and swim until we come to Green Land, where it's warm and green, and perhaps there we'll become green again."

The red leaf said to the yellow leaf:

"Right, let's do it."

They both landed on the river, and when they landed, the river didn't ripple, the way it does when kids throw pebbles or wood chips. That was because the leaves were very light, almost as light as feathers. The river felt only a caress on its back or perhaps just a tickle, because it wriggled like someone who's been tickled and said in its silvery voice:

"Hee-hee-hee!"

The leaves liked that. The yellow one called out to the red one:

"It's great on the river, delightful, even better than on a tree."

The red leaf said to the yellow leaf:

"Yes, it's just a little wet."

The yellow leaf said:

"Never mind that. We don't have to be afraid of water. Do you remember how the rain would often soak us on the tree?"

Talking this way, the two leaves floated farther and farther until the wind came and started to drive them back toward the bank from which they had just escaped.

So the leaves began to tremble, and the river itself trembled because the river, too, trembles from the wind. And the closer the leaves came to the bank, the more they shivered, because they did *not* want to go back to the ground and lie around in the autumn sludge.

But soon a wind came from the other side, and the two winds began to fight over the two leaves: the first wind chased the two leaves toward one bank, and the other wind chased them toward the other bank, so the two leaves never reached either side and continued floating in the middle of the river. The two winds fought and fought over the two leaves until they grew bored with the game and flew away, each to its cave, and the river became calm and still again. The leaves continued to float, as they'd intended.

They floated for a day, two, three, and four, and Green Land was still nowhere to be seen. So they floated on and on until the river flowed into a bigger river, and then they swam together with the bigger river until it began to flow into the sea. When the two leaves saw the vast sea with its frightening waves, which reached all the way up to the sky, they became very scared.

The red leaf called out to the yellow leaf:

"Let's go back, brother, because the sea will tear us apart. See how it roars and rages and swells?"

The yellow leaf said:

"Right, let's go back. I see now that it's a very long way to Green Land and that we'll never get there."

So the two leaves swam back, and they swam and swam until they returned to dry land, where it was autumn and where the wild winds blew.

But just then, a little girl standing on the riverbank saw the two leaves as they floated along. The two leaves looked very beautiful floating on the river, and the little girl liked them very much.

"What beautiful leaves!" said the little girl. "I'd love to have them!"

A wind heard this and gave a strong blow, driving the two leaves to the bank, where she could reach them. The little girl brought them home and thought about what she should do with them. She thought and thought until she remembered that she had a cousin in Green Land, so she said to herself, "I'll send her these two leaves, the yellow one and the red one, so that she can see what our land of winds and autumn does to green leaves. Mommy told me that in Green Land, everything is green, eternally green, and my cousin doesn't see leaves like these there."

So the little girl wrote a letter to her cousin in Green Land and enclosed the two leaves in the letter, the yellow one and the red one. The letter flew to Green Land over rivers and over seas. And when it arrived, it brought with it the two leaves, the yellow one and the red one.

The little girl in Green Land opened the letter and saw the two leaves—and she called to her mother:

"Look, Mama, what kinds of leaves grow in Autumn Land!"

But her mother explained to her that the leaves hadn't grown this way—this was how they fell.

The little girl in Green Land took the two leaves from Autumn Land and put them in a book as a keepsake. And the two leaves were pleased that at least they weren't lying around on the ground.

Translated by Lena Watson

BROKEN IN

Jacob Kreplak

1.

Recently, Hershele has become very suspicious. He doesn't ask anything or say anything, but goes around with his ears pricked up, his eyes anxious, and often looking expectantly into his mother's eyes.

He doesn't know for sure what it is, but his heart is telling him something's going to happen to him, something's gathering over his head.

He still plays all day long with the little peasant children in the village, near the wide, open river Seym. He runs around barefoot on the grassy bank, wades far into the overgrown, swampy ivy, or splashes for hours in the water and, using a small ball of bread tied to a thread, catches quivering silvery rudd.

Even now, he's playing . . . but a sense of fear won't

let him go. A sadness sits in his heart as if a shadow has slipped inside, cooling and darkening his youthful joy.

It all started when at home they began mentioning his name too many times and paying too much attention to him. Mama says something about him to Papa, and Papa says something about him to Mama, all in a way he doesn't quite understand. Mama, in particular, says a lot. With each stroke of his hair, with each "May your curly head be healthy," she asks him:

"Do you want to go to *heder*, Hershele? You do want to go to school, don't you?"

He doesn't reply. For some reason, his mother's questions make him sad. He doesn't know what to say. Why shouldn't he want to go to *heder* if, as Mama says, it's so good there? An angel throws kopecks, and children put on new shoes and pants with pockets and grow bigger. If the *heder* were in the village, he wouldn't let anyone rest until they took him there, and if they wouldn't, he'd run there all by himself. . . . And he'd show the angelic kopecks to Styopka and Mikita every day. They can't have them. He knows he's a Jewish boy and only Jewish boys are allowed in *heder*, but *heder* is some faraway place—where Uncle Elkanah lives. Hershele has seen his uncle only once and still remembers his beard, a strange big beard. Uncle Elkanah brought him a toy, and he remembers it well: a horse on wheels. He took it to the river for a drink and let it swim—just as old Mihalka does with his horse, Steely—and it floated away. He cried and screamed, so he was promised that when Uncle Elkanah came again, he'd bring him another horse. He asked every day, "Where's Uncle Elkanah? When is Uncle Elkanah coming?" Hershele was told that his uncle was already on his way.

But it's very, very far away, so he hasn't arrived yet.

His mother sees that he doesn't respond and understands him and looks at him with both pride and sadness.

"You're a smart boy! You want to go to *heder*. Will you go to Uncle Elkanah's? Do you want to go to your uncle's?"

"Yeah. . . ."

"Will you sleep at your uncle's?"

"With you in the same bed."

"And by yourself, in a good, soft bed?"

"No."

He doesn't leave his mother's side. When he's stuck at home because of bad weather, he trails after her from their home to the shop and from the shop back home. He goes behind the counter with her and follows her every move, often getting in his father's way. His father gets angry:

"Following her like a sheep! A five-year-old boy, who's starting *heder* soon, and still holding on to his mother's apron strings! Why are you always at our feet?"

But his mother always takes his side:

"What do you have against the child? He has to be somewhere. . . ."

At the river, he wades even farther into the swampy ivy and feels so strange in the tall, overgrown green flagroot that fully conceals him. It's cool and green there, green and cool—wonderfully green. At his slightest rustle, green frogs leap every which way—plop!—into the murky green water. And the smell of the flagroot is so strong, so sharp, so moist. . . . The water below bubbles up and gurgles. He places his bare feet carefully on the cool, swollen reddish-white ivy roots and, like a little hunting dog, scares colorful wild ducks and black moorhens.

He forgets about everything. His eyes light up: he'll catch one. Yet he's frightened every time a couple of ducks shoot up loudly from under his very feet and fly off lopsidedly across the river.

Here! A moorhen has sunk to the bottom like a pebble. He holds his breath. The ivy bends toward the water with him, the water bubbles up and gulps. His heart is pounding. He'll wait—he knows that the moorhen has to come up. The ivy leans closer and closer toward the water with him. Amid the bubbles, he sees another boy, and the water bubbles up, gulps, pulls—and he leans over closer and closer. . . .

But suddenly his heart trembles. He lifts his head and listens. It's as if someone's called him from the ivy:

"Hershele!"

Just like Mama. . . .

Sadness and longing take hold of him. He forgets about the moorhen and leaps out of the green-water world as quickly as possible.

Panting, he runs into the house.

"Where's Mama? Did you call me?"

"No, but I've been wondering where you were."

"Mama, I could've caught a moorhen. . . ."

"Just look at him!" grumbles his father. "The boy's going to *heder* soon and still has such nonsense on his mind."

Hershele catches his mother's sad gaze, and his heart sinks again in the face of the unknown.

2.

Overjoyed, Hershele runs into the shop and shouts in one breath:

"Mama, I've caught a pike hatchling, this tiny! I let him out in a little pool of water. . . ."

"May your curly head be healthy!" His mother showers him with kisses. "My darling boy, you."

"Come here, Hershel," his father interrupts. "Go to Mihalka and tell him to bring the wagon early tomorrow morning. Mama's taking you to your uncle's."

Any other time, going to see Mihalka—who'd mount Hershele on Steely and lead him back and forth across the farmyard—would make it a great day. From Steely's back the whole farmyard looks different, nothing like from down below. Now his heart sinks again: he senses his mother's wistful look beneath the kisses, and he keeps glancing anxiously, now at his earnest father, now at his mother.

"My smart boy, wait and see what a new pair of shoes we've bought you!"

3.

Dressed entirely in new clothes, Hershele sits with his mother on Mihalka's wagon and revels in the journey. It's a sunny day. On both sides of the ditch, the road stretches out like a string, together with the colorful autumnal forest. Colors play before his eyes: red, green, yellow, purple. Birds fly past, unlike any he's seen near the river. It smells of tree resin. There, from the depths of the forest, a mystery peeks out. And here, from time to time, they come across a wild pear tree with fruit, or a tree with unripe winter apples.

"Mama, I want to pick some apples."

"What do you need them for? They're no good. What for?"

"I want to. . . ."

Mama asks Mihalka, and he brings the wagon to a halt for a while.

Later, Hershele is even allowed to walk while the horse treads uphill, and he proudly walks in step with Mihalka, showing him that he's a big boy, picking wild-flowers in the ditch, running ahead and coming back.

Near a field of beanstalks Mihalka himself now stops the wagon again, lifts Hershele off so he can pick some beans—but not from the roots, he instructs him. Picking the roots is a sin.

Hershele has forgotten about everything. He delights in the new places, in the unfamiliar road. But at one point, catching sight of a fast-flowing silvery rivulet winding its way through a meadow, he throws up his hands.

"Oh, Mama, I left the pike hatchling in the pool. . . . He'll die." And he grows contemplative.

And later still he trembles again.

"Say, Haya," asks Mihalka in Ukrainian, "are you taking your little boy to *heder*?"

Hershele notices his mother winking to Mihalka to be quiet, and in Ukrainian Mihalka concludes: "Pity, still so little!" and gives a wave with his whip. "Giddyup!"

4.

Hershele arrives at Uncle Elkanah's as if in a daze. His head starts to spin.

Everything is completely different from their home, and there are lots of other children. It's extremely loud. Some of the kids play, others fight. They immediately encircle him, look at him with unfamiliar eyes, nearly pawing him, calling him to play.

He still keeps his distance, doesn't leave his mother's side for a minute.

His mother says:

"Go, play with the other children, Hershele. Why are you following me around, silly?"

And she begins to persuade him that he should go to *heder*, that he should listen to his aunt and uncle, be a good boy, listen to the teacher, and study intently—then everything would be fine. "Go, Hershele, play with the other kids. The teacher's coming soon. You're such a smart boy."

"Come, let's play buttons," the eldest child calls out to him. "We have a drawer full of buttons."

And suddenly he sees a whole drawer full of all sorts of buttons: bowl-shaped, porcelain, coins.

"I won this one," says one of the boys, and shows a bowl-shaped button in the palm of his hand. "It took me four goes."

"And I won this one."

"And I got this one."

Soon the game is in full swing. Hershele is a good, skillful flicker. He hits a button with one flick. He forgets about everything. Nothing interests him anymore except to win as many buttons as possible.

His mother brings some man over and says it's the teacher. The teacher pinches his cheek and says, "Oh, a precious, precious boy. Do you want to study?" He'd somehow imagined a teacher looking altogether different—this one looks just like all the other people who come to visit.

He says, "I do," but only to be able to go back to the game: he was about to win a "bowl." So what if that's the teacher. . . .

He notices his mother whispering, now to his aunt,

now to his uncle—no response. Mihalka comes in, whip in hand, and stands in the doorway—no response. His mother comes up as he lies on the floor playing, kisses him and smiles—no response. He hears a wagon drive off outside—no response. Suddenly he trembles, tosses the buttons, and flies out into the yard. . . .

His aunt tries to grab him by the hand but doesn't succeed. His uncle stands there, at a loss, with half-formed words on his lips.

"What—what are you running for?"

By then, Hershele's already outside. He sees the wagon with his mother turn into a side street, and with a shout—"Mama!"—he bolts after the wagon with all his might.

He sees nothing, feels nothing. People seem to be stopping and calling out to him, "What's the matter, little boy?" He tries to dodge them. And the wagon keeps driving away faster. . . .

In desperation, he runs with all his might, and his terrified call—"Mama!"—breaks out more and more frequently. He wants to collapse sobbing, but his little legs run all by themselves, and his heart tears the air apart.

"Ma-ma-aa, take me with you!"

But the wagon is far, far away. . . .

Suddenly he sees his mother turn her head to him and gesture, now to him, and now to Mihalka. It seems she's telling Mihalka to drive faster while gesturing to Hershele to go back. . . . And he sprints, stretching out his arms.

"Mama, take me with you! Take me with you!"

He sees the wagon stop, his mother gets out. He strains to run even faster toward her, and she runs to meet him. He is now lying cradled in her arms, the words "Mama, take me with you!" still pouring forth from his throat.

His mother wipes off his sweaty brow, snuggles him to herself, and says:

"You're a bad boy. I thought you promised to be good and listen. . . . Mihalka, drive back to his uncle's. . . ."

Back at his uncle's, everyone scolds him, both his aunt and his uncle, but the children look differently at him and don't interfere in anything. He doesn't care. He clings to his mother like a lamb, holds on to her dress and doesn't leave her side. She no longer attempts to leave him. When she puts him to bed, she has to sit by his side and he holds her hand.

He wakes up with a start, his eyes shutting tight from the sun, looks wildly around, and starts to call in desperation, "Mama! Where's Mama?" He receives no answer, but his uncle comes in and says, "Shh, shh, Mama's coming soon."

He asks nothing else and quietly lets his head drop. His eyes well up. The room and everything in it begin to move away from him and become distorted. For the first time, he sees the world through real tears.

A few days later, Hershele starts *heder*. The angel throws him kopecks. He takes pride in his new pants with pockets, and plays buttons.

Translated by Lena Watson

THE MOON AND THE LITTLE BOY

Leon Elbe

One night, taking a lonely stroll around the sky, the moon all at once grew sad. It thought: "Why don't I wake up one of the boys or girls—I'll have someone to play with and will feel better."

The moon peeked into every window. Here it saw a boy sleeping and there a girl sleeping, but they were sleeping so soundly that there was no way to wake them. The moon tried to tickle this boy and that girl with a ray of light but could only get them to smile in their sleep. They slept so peacefully and so beautifully that they were even a delight to watch.

The moon grew sadder and sadder as it strolled around all alone at night in such a big, wide world. It thought: "How good the sun must have it! It's happy. It has people to play with all day long. All the children are on the street, and the sun plays with them. In the evening, the sun leaves to go to sleep, and the children, too, go to sleep. When I appear and the children are already in bed, and I have no one to play with. And when the children wake up, I have to go to bed already! Ugh! It's no fun being a moon and staying awake all night while everyone is asleep, and sleeping all day while everyone is awake."

The moon moved on and on and peeked into all the windows and tried its luck in case somewhere there was a boy or a girl who wasn't sleeping. Or maybe somewhere there was a boy or a girl it could waken, and then it would have someone to play with. But again it had no luck: all the children slept deeply, and it couldn't wake them up.

The moon then begged the children to get up and play with it. In return, it would give them belts of silver light-rays that would be even more beautiful than the sun's belts of gold. It begged and begged. . . .

Children sleeping tight,
Children unaware.
No one wants to wake,
No one seems to care.

When the moon saw that its begging wasn't helping, because the children slept so deeply and couldn't hear anything, it tickled them again. Maybe one of the children wouldn't be able to bear it and would wake up anyway?

It tickled one boy with its rays, and it tickled his eyes for so long that he really couldn't bear it and he squeezed his eyes tight. He squeezed and squinted for so long that he woke up and opened his eyes. The boy looked around and wanted to know who'd tickled him. He looked and looked and couldn't find anyone—Mama and Papa were sleeping, and no one else was in the room. The moon stood there, peeking into the window and choking with laughter.

The boy noticed the moon and asked: "Was it you who tickled me?"

The moon answered: "Of course it was! Can't you see that everyone's sleeping and I'm the only one awake?"

The boy asked it: "Why did you tickle me?"

The moon answered: "Because I wanted you to get up and play with me—because I'm bored being alone all night."

The boy said: "Fine, I'll play with you." He began to play with the moon. From her sleep, his mother heard that he was no longer sleeping, and she got up to ask her son: "Why aren't you asleep? Why aren't you in bed?"

The boy answered: "The moon . . ." And he pointed at the window.

The mother glanced at the window and saw the moon—a full and smiling moon.

"Aha!" she said. "The moon won't let you sleep! I'll show it!"

The mother walked behind the bed and pulled down the thick window curtains. The moon couldn't peek in anymore, and the room was so dark that you couldn't see a thing. At first the boy refused to accept that the moon had been taken from him, and he tossed and turned in his bed unhappily for a long time. In the end, he fell back asleep.

The moon left his window, embarrassed, and went to another window. And there it saw another boy. That boy happened not to be asleep, and neither was his mother. The boy's mother was sitting next to him. She caressed him and spoke to him with such gentle words that it was pleasant to listen to her.

The moon peeked into the window, and just as it peeked in, the mother said: "Look, my dear, it's the moon!"

The moon wondered why the boy's mother wasn't shooing it away from the window, as the other boy's mother had done. On the contrary, pointing to the moon, this boy's mother said to him: "Look, my dear, what a beautiful moon! See how it's looking at us and smiling? Can you see the little man in the moon? Can you see the nose and the mouth and the eyes?"

The moon was astonished and happy that the boy's mother praised it. But suddenly it heard the boy groan. The mother asked him: "Where does it hurt, my dear? Is your head still hurting?"

The boy nodded ever so slightly and with difficulty said: "Yes. . . ."

The moon understood that the boy was sick. It took pity on him and inched its face closer to the window. It caressed the boy with its rays, and he began to feel better and smile. The mother, too, smiled.

"See, my dear?" she said to him. "The moon's playing with you. Play with it, play, my dear, play, and you'll feel better."

The moon tried even harder to caress the sick boy with its rays, and the mother, too, caressed him. For a while, the boy was more cheerful and happy. The moon laughed and he laughed, and this way they played together all night long. At dawn, the moon parted with the boy and went to bed. The boy fell asleep, too, and slept well into the day.

He got up and his head no longer hurt. He was healthy again and asked his mother for food. She gave him food and he ate everything. He sat down on the floor and played with his toys.

At night, the moon returned to play with the boy, but he was already asleep and it didn't want to disturb him.

"Let him sleep," the moon thought. "The poor thing didn't sleep last night—he wasn't well. Let him sleep tonight!"

The moon hid behind a cloud so that it wouldn't disturb the boy's sleep.

He woke up once, and the moon emerged for a short while with its kind and sweet smile. The boy smiled, too, and fell back asleep. The moon moved away from the window and hid again behind a cloud.

Translated by Sandra Chiritescu

REBELLION

THE LITTLE BOY WITH THE SAMOVAR

Jacob Reisfeder

There once lived a ruler who waged war against so many nations, aiming to take their lands, that he started running out of rifles for his soldiers. There was not even enough brass or lead in the land to make bullets.

The ruler began worrying as the other nations banded together and prepared to move on his land. And he wasn't one to surrender.

He delivered a decree to his people, stating that in three days' time, they all had to turn in any lead, copper, or brass metalware that could be found in their homes. And, out of fear, everyone brought their metalware, on their own, to the places where it was being collected.

Among the poor people lived a quiet and graceful little boy with blond hair and blue eyes that were unusually lovely and intelligent. He was a curious boy who wanted to know everything in the world. He would look at each thing for a long time and think: "Where does that stream end up?" "What do those clouds way up high float toward?" "How do birds build their nests?" "How do flowers grow in the fields?" "And how is bread made, the bread I eat each and every day?"

He also liked eavesdropping on adult conversations, and so none of them could stand him. But worst of all were his strange questions: "Why do some children walk around ragged and barefoot in the cold, while other children get to wear fancy coats and pants?" "What about the pretty dolls, toy horses, and booklets that fill the shops—who are they for if poor children, who long for them so dearly, can never have them?" "Why are some people poor and others rich?" "Wouldn't it be better if everyone were equal?" Endless questions . . .

This little boy had a small, lovely toy brass samovar—artfully made and decorated with red silk ribbons and fringed paper streamers—which his parents had bought him as a present for his fifth birthday. That was already two years ago—the boy was now seven years old. But the samovar was as good as new. It stood by the window on a special little table and shone in the sun like gold, so often did the little boy clean and polish it. It was his favorite toy of all the beautiful things he had.

He loved imagining how his friends would come over, and the samovar would boil and steam, and he would pour tea for each of them from his own little samovar into his own little cups, and they would all drink and enjoy feeling like grown-ups.

This is how the little boy played with his samovar and took care of it—as if it were the apple of his eye.

While the copper and brass metalware was being collected from all the houses throughout the land, the little boy listened in silence and grief to the grown-up conversations about how the metalware would be used. He walked around quietly with tears in his eyes and an ache in his heart.

He thought about his papa, who'd gone off to be killed in the war. He'd kissed the little boy and left, never to return.

"What for?" thought the sorrowful boy. "Had he ever harmed anyone? He was such a good papa."

The morning when his mother gathered all the metalware in the house and prepared to take it away, she cast a glance at the samovar, but was overcome with pity for her child. . . . She knew only too well what the samovar meant to him, how unhappy she would make him if she took it away. But neither could she leave it there, because if she were later found to have it, she'd be severely punished. The ruler was a hot-tempered person, and his guards had not a single glimmer of mercy in their hearts.

So she reached out her hand to take the samovar. But the little boy threw himself onto the toy, clasped it tight with both hands, and cried out, beside himself: "No! . . . No! . . . No! . . . I won't let you take my samovar! . . . I won't let you!" And he stamped his feet and threw himself around, as if in a fit.

His mother took pity on her only child and left the samovar in his hands. "At least hide it so that it won't be found," she entreated him.

The little boy hid his precious samovar in a good, safe place. But he'd take it out from time to time, whenever he was overcome with the desire to play with it.

One day, the city guards went from house to house to see whether any metalware had not been turned in. They entered the little boy's house unexpectedly, right when he was playing with his brass samovar next to the window.

"Hey, you bad little boy!" they roared. "Playing with brass, are you?! You'd better stick to playing with the streamers, and we'll put the samovar to better use. Now hand it over—quick!"

The little boy flung his arms around the samovar and

clutched it with extraordinary strength. He pleaded with the angry guards: "Have pity on me, don't take away my samovar!"

"You can play with something else!" yelled the guards.

"I'd just as well play with nothing at all," cried the little boy. "But I won't give up the samovar. I know exactly what you'll do with it!" And the boy burst out into such wails that even the guards were moved by his tears.

"But there's nothing to be done, little boy," they said, stroking his hair. "We're powerless. Our ruler has decreed that everyone in the land must give up all their copper and brass."

"So take me to the ruler," the little boy blurted out. "I'll ask him to stop ordering you to take away my samovar."

The guards smiled and, for curiosity's sake, took him to their officer. The officer laughed when he heard the little boy's request. He sent the boy to his own superior—and so it went until the little boy was at last given an audience with the ruler himself.

The ruler had heard about the matter that the little boy had come to discuss. He addressed the boy with a smile: "What good is the samovar to you, little boy? I will decree that you shall receive other toys instead, much prettier toys than your samovar."

"I don't need any toys to play with," the little boy answered. "I can do without."

"So then why do you refuse to give up the samovar?" the interested ruler asked.

The little boy burst into tears and in a choked voice cried out, "Because I don't want my samovar to be used to make bullets that will kill someone else's papa—the way my papa was killed." And he wept even more bitterly.

The little boy's words sent chills down the ruler's spine. He bent his head and pondered. Then he lifted the child onto his lap and kissed his forehead warmly.

"You dear, wise little boy! No—your samovar will never be taken away."

The ending was as happy as could be. Thanks to the little boy's words—which had touched the ruler so deeply—he issued a decree that very day, ordering all metalware to be returned to its rightful owners. It was no longer needed because the ruler had realized, at last, that too much blood had been spilled—and that there could finally be an end to all war.

Translated by Ri J. Turner and David Stromberg

THE KING WHO LICKED HONEY

Moyshe Nadir

In Khoyrez Land, there was a king who ruled only on Mondays and Thursdays. On Tuesdays, Wednesdays, Fridays, and the Sabbath, he didn't rule at all. On Sundays, he would sometimes stop by to work for an hour or two at his kingship, quickly rule about something, and go home to wash up—all before sitting to lick honey out of a jar.

In Khoyrez Land, no one knew that the king ruled so little—that the kingship stood vacant five days a week and that people were paying its rent for nothing. Neither did anyone know that the king was licking honey out of a jar since he did it ever so secretly. The king's servants would lower the curtains, turn out the lights, bolt the locks, lure all the shadows into a sack, and shake it out outside. Then the Royal Chamberlain would yell out, "And-all-a-mar-shack-y," and this was a sign that the king could now stick his tongue into the jar and lick away.

But a human being is nothing more than a human being.

And the world isn't asleep.

And walls have ears.

So it was found out. How was it found out? I'll tell you.

The clever people of Khoyrez Land sent in a spy, who snuck in a jar with a narrow lid. What did the king know? A jar's a jar. First he shoved a finger inside (as the oldest kings of Khoyrez Land had done) and tasted it. Sweet? Sweet. He didn't ask any questions and shoved his tongue inside, and—*me-ee*—he couldn't pull it back out.

The King of Khoyrez stomped around his palace. The jar swung from his mouth, and he wanted to say something but couldn't.

The sages were rounded up with a whip, the stargazers were called together with a piercing whistle, and they were all told:

"The king can't take his tongue out of the jar. Do something! It's not good for a king to go around with a jar hanging off his tongue."

The sages and stargazers started rubbing their foreheads with their fists, until they nearly rubbed holes into them—but they couldn't think of anything. They grabbed their long beards with their hands and brought them up closer to their eyes, looking in their beards to see if they could maybe find something *there*, but it was useless.

A full day and a night, the sages and the stargazers sat and thought and thought, and thought of nothing. Then they drank coffee with sweet cream and still they thought of nothing. Then they ate some canned peaches—and still they thought of nothing.

On the third day, a court messenger came and said:

"Any sages and stargazers who cannot figure out how to save the king will have to roll peas with their noses across the entire city, back and forth, and those who refuse will be hanged!"

Seven elderly sages rolled peas with their noses. The others, in the meantime, sat and thought about how to save the king.

"Hey, you know what?" called one of the stargazers. "Let's lay the king down outside, put an anvil underneath his tongue, give it a whack with a hammer, and break the jar."

"And what will happen to the tongue?" asked a sage.

"The tongue?" said the stargazer. "The tongue is a serious problem."

"Ba, ba, ba—if only there was no tongue?!" said the elderly sage, and shoved a little pea along with his nose. . . .

"Perhaps," cut in a slightly stuttering sage, "perhaps if we kn-knocked out the k-k-king's t-t-teeth, he c-c-could hold the j-j-jar ins-side his m-mouth, and n-no one w-would kn-kn-know it was there."

The sages and stargazers looked around. The seven who had been rolling peas produced little laughs and continued to sweep the earth with their beards—and no other suggestions were made.

Meanwhile, all across Khoyrez Land, the rumor spread that the king was licking honey—so this was one thing! And that, having licked honey, it hadn't done the poor guy any good—and this was a second thing! And anyway, how was it that he got to lick honey and his people didn't? And this was a third thing!

The republicans immediately started sharpening their knives and went off to the king. And their leader kicked with his foot and yelled in German, in a rough voice, to scare the king:

"Where do you keep the thrrrrone?"

"D'thro wite-eer!" answered the king with the jar on his tongue.

(That's to say, "The throne's right here!")

"Shake it up," the leader ordered the other republicans. "It's time for the throne to shake!"

They started shaking the throne back and forth until they broke one of its legs. When they did, they calmed down and left to eat pancakes with butter.

As the republicans left, the democrats appeared, yelling and waving their hands.

"Where's the king? What's this supposed to mean—the king's licking honey and we aren't?"

"Nah yih cah thee huh buthy I'th bihn," yelled the king, which is to say: "Now you can see how busy I've been!"

"Busy or not," yelled the assemblyman from the Thirty-Ninth District, "all this time, you've been licking honey—and we haven't!"

The king went onto his porch and gathered his in-laws, the head steward of his royal butcher knives, and all the sages and stargazers. And the king held forth with the following speech, the jar on his tongue:

"Fliends and cidy folk,

"We havl all come togeler wil da pulpose of conthidering the sidualion in oul kinlgdom. I delieve, my fliends and cidy folk, tlat dere ilsn't duch to thay. . . . Il id tlue, my fliends, tlat I havl licked hodey, dut look at wlat all dis licking hath blought me. . . ."

When the king's in-laws and the head steward of his royal butcher knives and the sages and stargazers heard his speech, they all let out a painful cry, and they cried out an entire sea. And the king sat himself down in a ship and set out into the world—with the jar on his tongue and with the taste of past honey-filled days between his yellowing teeth, which protruded from under a thick, calf-like lip.

Translated by David Stromberg

THE KINGDOM OF ANTS AND MUSHROOMS

Sonya Kantor

Far, far off, in strange and distant lands, stood a deep, thick, dark forest. The trees and bushes were so overgrown that no one could pass through. The forest was full of animals—wolves, bears, foxes—each living in their own dens and burrows.

In the hollows of ancient trees lived red squirrels, and at the forest's edge, tiny young rabbits plucked fresh shoots and buds from the trees.

And there were so many birds in the forest! From earliest dawn, it was filled with the unceasing sound of their singing and chirping.

And don't even ask how many flowers grew in that forest! Insects and flies came from far and wide to collect the sweet nectar from the flowers.

And in the middle of the forest, in a grassy clearing, stood the kingdom of mushrooms. A powerful old mushroom ruled the kingdom. He was cracked from old age and was even a little worm-eaten, but the mushrooms admired him and followed his rule because he was wise and good.

Every time it rained, he'd command:

"Milk caps—take cover under the pines. Chantrelles, yellow knights—hide under the bushes. Scaberstalks—don't scatter across the forest, stay together! And what's this? Get those crazy fly-traps out of here! All dressed up in red dresses and white pearls, full of themselves and good for nothing."

Each and every day, different types of worms, flies, and birds visited the kingdom. The mushrooms lived in peace with everyone. However, they got along best with the ants, who would often come to the green mushroom kingdom to collect ladybugs.

Not far from the forest clearing, under an old, moldering pine tree, was their queendom, a great anthill. It was ruled by females—the queens—and not just one but many. The queens were also very wise, and every day they toiled and worked hard.

Their anthill had several levels, with many chambers, storerooms, and corridors—long and short, wide and narrow, twisty and straight.

Early each morning, the queens would divide up the work:

"*You* sisters, go and make our palace bigger—it'll be time to lay fresh eggs soon. *You* sisters must protect the eggs until they develop into respectable ants. Take them out into fresh air if it's a nice day out, bring them back inside when it gets cold and rainy. *You,* my dear sisters, must provide us all with food. Bring us May bugs, earthworms, and milk. We need milk in our storerooms today. And what's this? Drones? Drive those loafers out from our palace! They do nothing but fly around in the sunshine empty-handed."

The workers and their queens lived well. Everyone worked—both the queens, who could fly, and the ordinary workers, who had no wings. But anyone who didn't work was cast out from the palace forever.

On holidays, when the sun's heat baked the earth, the ants would go to visit the green mushroom kingdom. Not everyone would go. The heads of households had to stay home to protect their belongings.

Arriving at the mushrooms' forest clearing, the ants would sit down. "So what's new?" the mushrooms would ask. "Tell us!"

"Today I cast out my son," an ant queen said one day.

"Can you imagine such a lazy drone!? We work all day long, and we love our work—and that loafer doesn't want to work, he just plays and flies around in the sun!"

The old mushroom king contemplated this sadly.

"Yes, yes. If I had a son, I don't think I would be able to cast him out. I'd try to do everything possible to make him into someone respectable! But I have no son. I have none, my dear friends!"

The ants nodded with their long antennae, but they saw things differently: "Our sons are not respectable, they do not want to work, and lazy drones must be driven out."

Not always had the king been childless. Long ago, he'd had yellow, brown, and white mushroom children, daughters and sons. Unfortunately, they hadn't grown well. Some rotted, grew worm-eaten, and died. The others were trampled by wild animals.

Be that as it may, the king now had no heir.

The visit wasn't long. Work in the anthill couldn't wait.

And so the two kingdoms lived in peace.

The summer passed, and it began to rain for a week, then two, then three. The rains soaked everything through, down to the hiddenmost mushroom spores. After the rains passed, the sun came out.

The king awoke one beautiful morning, looked around, and could not believe his eyes: a son! A beautiful, healthy, fresh, and moist mushroom looked back at him tenderly.

Soon the happy news spread across the entire forest. Lilies, dandelions, and wild bellflowers sang together and rang out with great joy. Two summer insects, a gnat and a cricket, invited everyone to the great feast. All the worms promised to watch over the young prince all day and all night and protect him from evildoers.

The message arrived at the anthill very late. Imagine the preparations the ants made! First they went to the narrow river that flowed nearby, and washed off all the dust, each ant helping its neighbor. Then they set out. A large part of the forest, near the anthill and around some of the clearing turned black with ants. And look at all the guests who'd come! There wasn't room for a pin, the forest clearing was so crowded. Mosquitoes and flies, bees and butterflies, even an orchestra! Crickets and horseflies, owls and cuckoos, and a colorful woodpecker to drum a beat.

And the crowd began to dance. The May bugs flew around at a distance, for though the mushrooms had invited them, they were afraid of the ants.

The celebration was in full swing when suddenly a

wild bee arrived. Terrified and breathless, she sat on a tall linden tree and shrieked:

"Something terrible has happened! A misfortune for the forest!"

"What happened? Tell us!" Everyone made a dash toward the bee.

"Bad news, my friends: A new forest keeper has moved into the forest with two children. You've never seen naughtier children in your life. They run around the forest all day, picking berries, plucking flowers, breaking the young bushes."

The old mushroom king thought for a while. Then he smiled and said to the bee:

"My dear, wise friend, you exaggerate. So what if they tear off a few berries and gather flowers? That causes no harm. The flowers won't bear a grudge against the children. They use them to weave beautiful crowns."

The bee was hurt.

"Sure—you didn't see how they picked the flowers, so you don't know. Wait and see what tune you sing when they start to pick your own kind. It's easy for you to say this now—just a few berries, a few flowers," buzzed the furious bee. "It's not just a few. They're tearing and picking and ruining everything. They catch butterfies and tear off their wings. They pester the ants."

"The ants?" the queens cried in fear. "Sisters, come. Let's return to our palace!"

"They're not sparing the mushrooms, either!" the bee buzzed quietly.

"The mushrooms, too?" All the mushrooms let out a sad gasp.

"Yes, dear friends. So what do you say now?"

But she was unable to finish.

They heard the sound of a chase. The earth trembled, branches cracked, and two pretty children's heads appeared among the overgrown bushes.

"Look at all the flowers! Look at all these mushrooms growing here. Let's pick them!" cried out Sheyndele.

"Pick them yourself. I'd rather catch flies!" And Hershele started chasing the flies with cries of joy.

He ran and ran until he suddenly saw something that made him stop in wonder. Hordes of terrified ants were running to their palace. Hershele had never seen so many insects in his life. "A real army," he thought, looking at the orderly rows of marching ants.

Hershele stopped to think. He climbed onto something that resembled a little hill.

Ants—terrified and startled—came pouring out from all sides. Without realizing it, Hershel had climbed onto their palace and destroyed its uppermost level.

Afraid of the ants, who streamed out of the anthill and rushed straight toward the destroyer, Hershele dashed back to the spot where he'd left Sheyndele.

Sheyndele, meanwhile, had been plucking mushrooms. The old king looked on with a trembling heart. His son, his only consolation! Perhaps she wouldn't notice him. . . .

Sheyndele, however, saw the fresh mushroom. She plucked him and left him lying on the ground—there was no more room left in her basket.

"Come on, Hershel, let's go home!"

The children left. It grew quiet in the forest. The sun set. The old king stood silently by his dead son, and tears trickled slowly down his wrinkled face.

And not far from the forest clearing, the ants began to pick up their crushed sisters and console them:

"Don't cry, my dears, don't cry, my loves. In the morning, we'll start building a new palace."

Translated by Debra Caplan

THE WISE HAT

Moyshe Nadir

1.

Children, would you like to hear a story about a wise little hat? Let me tell you about it:

There once lived an emperor named Yuhavit the Great. He was called "Yuhavit" because after almost every third word, he'd say, "There you have it." And he was called "the Great" because he was so little, a real nothing, with thick feet and a belly that he shoved forward going "ep-hu." And so he wanted people to call him nothing other than "the Great."

In short, Emperor Yuhavit the Great ruled over many lands full of soldiers, taxes, cholera every summer, typhus every winter—so plenty going on!

Just like any other emperor, Emperor Yuhavit ruled "by someone else's hand." He himself preferred to eat the best of foods and to drink them down with the finest of wines, which were so old that the jars in which the wine was kept would be dead drunk and dance around between one cellar and another—you could hardly catch them.

The kingdom was managed by two ministers: Meshgig, the court sage, and Getzim, the court fool. Meshgig the Sage took care of the kingdom's businesses, composed documents whenever necessary, got mad at everyone, and sucked your soul dry. Getzim the Fool would make the ministers and military men and tax collectors laugh with all his foolishness so that they had the strength to do what Meshgig the Sage required of them.

With such a sage for a court minister, Emperor Yuhavit could, as can be imagined, sleep quietly. What does "quietly" mean? He slept so soundly that he could be awakened only by whistling into his ear through the throat of a freshly butchered goose.

The emperor would slowly wake up, first letting his right eye be rubbed, then his left. He instructed his High Yawner to yawn for him. Then—with a kind of cannon the sage had invented—he would have his pants and jacket and medals shot onto him, and the emperor would scratch himself, saying, "There you have it! Yet another Monday!" And he would go have breakfast.

Emperor Yuhavit the Great never had to worry about anything or pinch any pennies.

2.

Meshgig's name was known all over the world, and Getzim's name was also known throughout the nations. But while Meshgig was recognized as a great sage, Getzim was considered just as big of a blockhead.

What no one—including Meshgig himself—knew was that Meshgig's wisdom was not in his head but in his hat.

This very hat was made from the skin of a dwarf, and whoever put it on became the greatest sage in the world.

How Meshgig came upon this hat . . . is a story of its own. For now, all we need to know is that the difference between the greatest sage and the greatest fool is only in the hat. One has a foolish hat, and the other—we already said.

A story like this once decided to happen:

In a bet between our emperor and another emperor about whose minister was a greater sage, the two wisest people from each nation were locked up in a single hall to see what would happen.

Everyone waited three days and three nights. On the morning of the fourth day, people heard a shriek, and Meshgig, the greatest of all sages, flew out of the locked hall without a hat, a little bloody around the nose and between the teeth.

When Getzim the Fool, who stood watch just outside, saw this, he ran inside screaming:

"Hey there, what's this about, taking a sage and hitting him and snatching his hat?"

But four minutes later, he also flew back, a little bloody. And through the windows of the closed hall, *two* hats came flying.

When the sage saw this, he was very embarrassed, grabbed the first hat that his hand could reach, and ran off to the emperor to tell him what had happened: the other sage had been violent.

Knowing the kind of person he had on his hands, the emperor let go a little yawn, gave a "There you have it," and ordered the wise Meshgig to write a letter to the other emperor, saying that his sage had been violent and telling him in the strictest of terms that if he did not immediately send a wagonful of saffron, eleven barrels of cinnamon, two hundred pounds of pickled peas-and-things, and eighteen barrels of diamonds—it would cost him dearly.

"Well—start writing!" said the emperor to the sage. "You know how!"

But the sage sat with his tongue sticking out, picking his nose, and understanding nothing of what was said to him.

"There you have it!" said Emperor Yuhavit the Great. "Now stop picking your nose. You can't do that if you're a sage!"

"Really?" said the sage, and bubbled up with a little laugh. "Who says?"

The emperor looked at him sideways and said:

"Why are you pretending to be a fool? Start writing!"

"Me? I should write?" asked the sage, and started laughing mischievously. "What do you want I should write? I should ask if his woodpecker is still coughing? I just don't know what to write. . . ."

"Stop pretending you're a fool!" The emperor got fired up. "Here. Take this quill in your hand and write!" And into the sage's hand, he put a large goose quill.

Meshgig licked it, smiled, poured half a bottle of ink onto a new piece of parchment, wiped it clean with the sleeve of his expensive purple wool coat, and started writing:

Greetings, dear Emperor,

First, I'm writing to say that we're, thank God, in the best of health, and may God grant that we hear the same from you. Second, I'm writing you, dear Emperor, to say that my emperor has angrily told me to write you a wise missive, and so I'm writing you this wise missive, and asking you to let me know—what date does Shushan Purim fall on for you over there? And there's no other news to write about—because my emperor is looking at me a little angrily. It's possible that he might give me a smack, too.

As the emperor read the missive, he put out his hand and—*trask! flem!*—one, two, three, four . . .

The sage covered his face, held on to his hat, and laughed so foolishly that the emperor also started laughing. Soon the ministers, including the court fool, all gathered together and stood at the threshold—laughing, too.

Everyone laughed except the fool. He stood serious, with great pride and dignity. He had his right hand on his sword, and his eyes looked sharp and wise.

"There you have it!" said the emperor, and pointed to the sage, who sat on the ground carving something into the foot of the throne with a penknife. "Our sage is so wise he's become a fool. Now we're, God forbid, lost for good. . . . What should we do?"

"What to do," said the fool, counting every word as if it were a pearl. "We take and we . . ."

He said nothing else out loud. He just whispered in the emperor's ear. The emperor was startled—he slammed his hand down—and then he said, "We've been saved." And he ordered that the fool should be made the court sage.

The courtiers quickly fulfilled the emperor's orders. They anointed the fool with oil, covered him with perfume, plied him with fragrant herbs, dressed him in royal attire, and took him out to the palace balcony. And the Minister of the Most Internal Affairs disclosed to the people, who had gathered in the thousands:

"People! There's been a miracle! The greatest fool has suddenly become the greatest sage. . . . You yourself will hear him speak and see for yourself."

The former fool walked onto the balcony, made a deep bow, and was about to say something. But he had, it seemed, bowed too deeply, because his hat fell off and he was left standing, like a clay golem, scratching his head with his pinky finger. After some thought, he finally blurted out: "A good Sabbath!" (It was actually Wednesday.)

By the next day, a revolution began. Emperor Yuhavit was decapitated. The former fool, who remained a fool, was hanged. The former sage, who had now also become a fool, was shot. Their clothing and their hats were destroyed. And now everything is as it should be.

Translated by David Stromberg

THE DIAMOND PRINCE

Jacob Reisfeder

Off in a certain land there once lived a king. He was a giant who was strong enough to knock down walls. He had conquered half the world, and the kings he had conquered would follow behind his golden wagon and kneel before him.

And the queen—she was as beautiful as an angel. Her eyes were bluer than heaven and brighter than the sun, and her golden locks were more beautiful than the diamond crown she wore on her head.

Yet the king was unhappy, and he envied the poorest beggar whom God had blessed with a child.

"What good is all this to me?" he would think as he wandered all alone in his garden, which had a silvery stream running through it and golden fruits growing, and songbirds twittering sweetly and playing among the branches.

What good was it to be a great man if he was so bereft and lonely? . . . All his amusements, all his kingly pleasures, had become tedious to him, and even his beautiful queen could no longer lift his spirits. He would give away entire lands, he would even give up years of his life, if only the queen could make him happy with a child.

And in the crystal palace, in the loveliest golden hall, the beautiful queen spent her days with tears pouring from her bright eyes, begging God for a child so that she could provide the king with his heart's desire. All the holy people from the farthest lands in the kingdom had beseeched God endlessly on behalf of the royal couple, and sorcerers had given all kinds of advice and blessed the king and queen hundreds of times. But nothing helped. The beautiful queen was not favored with a child, and the young king went around looking pensive and mournful, unable to take pleasure in anything.

One day, a very old sorceress arrived at the royal palace after a long journey from a faraway land. There, in her decrepit hut at the tip of a magical mountain, she had heard of the great king's sadness and the queen's weeping, and her witch's heart quivered with sympathy. So she locked up her hut with seven locks and set forth—leaning on black crutches and carrying two strange, thick sticks—to help the suffering king and queen.

And when the king and queen learned why the sorceress had come, they ran over to greet her, and both of them kissed the thin, dirty fingers of her witch's hands and beseeched her with tears in their eyes: "Help us, venerable sorceress, help us!"

When the shrunken, hideous, centuries-old sorceress saw the great king and the most beautiful queen in the world kneel down before her, she was deeply moved, and she covered her clouded old eyes with her dirty hands and wept with strange, squeaky sobs.

But soon she wiped her witch's eyes, steadied herself on her black crutches, looked around the sumptuous golden hall, peered at the crystal panes and into every corner, muttered something from between her blue lips, and waved one of her strange, thick sticks in the air— and suddenly the golden light of day disappeared and the hall was illuminated by a red glow.

And the sorceress in her many-colored rags lifted her long hands above the crowns of the king and queen and blessed them with the first words that came to her mind:

"May you have a bright son—a diamond of a son! Let the beauty of all the worlds shine out from his eyes. Let him have the strongest arms of all the sons in the land. Let his voice be so like the voice of a songbird that he will bewitch every listener with his divine singing, and let his mind be filled with the wisdom of the entire world!"

And, children, the old sorceress's words were full of magic, and she pronounced them at an auspicious moment.

At the end of the year, the queen truly did bear a son.

"My God! What a child! Made of diamonds!" the elder midwife exclaimed when she caught her first glimpse of the infant crown prince. She squinted against the blinding rays that poured from the child, filling the hall with a sea of light.

"A marvel!" cried the second midwife, stumbling back in wonder. "Just look at him! His whole body is made of diamonds!"

"Truly—what a child! Like a picture!" Disbelief rippled through the ranks of the assistant midwives.

The queen overheard their talk, and ordered the midwives to show her the child. As soon as she saw him, she trembled and turned very pale. Out of fear lest an evil eye be cast on the wondrous child, she swore the midwives to secrecy, so that no one in the land would find out. In addition, she decreed that among the dozens of servants in the palace, only the youngest ones would be allowed to see the child and take care of him.

The joy of the king and queen knew no bounds.
Nevertheless, they were worried—the child's extraordinary beauty, and the diamond glow that emanated from
him, frightened them a little. . . .

In the meantime, the child grew, and his radiant diamond limbs grew strong and healthy. He was a giant and
disliked being fussed over. At the first chance, he'd run
out of the palace into the garden, to unusually beautiful
trees laden with golden fruits, and to the silvery stream,
at which he loved to gaze through the palace windows.

The sweet songs that would occasionally burst from
his throat when he was playing with his young caretakers
entranced anyone who heard him and put the best court
singers to shame. And the king's grizzled-gray old advi-
sors gaped at the boy's extraordinary wisdom, and more
than once found themselves disconcerted by his remark-
ably clever questions.

So you see, children, all the pronouncements of the
old sorceress were fulfilled.

But once, while the crown prince was playing excit-
edly in the garden with his caretakers, he crossed paths
with several of the courtiers' children. These were the
first children the crown prince had ever seen. And when
the other children saw the crown prince's diamond
face, they drew nearer and stood in a circle around him,

pointing and staring with astonished, curious eyes. They called out to their own caretakers: "Oh my, what a face he has! Ha-ha-ha, it's blinding. I can't keep my eyes on him. . . ."

And the crown prince stopped in his tracks, ashamed. He turned his big blue eyes toward the ground and silently, sadly dragged his caretakers away from the other children. And when he went back inside the palace, he stole away to one of the side rooms and stood for a long time before a large golden mirror, looking with shame at his own bright face, which was as blinding as a little sun.

"What kind of face do I have, anyway?" he wondered for the first time, and was immediately disheartened. All the other children had a different kind of face—they had such soft, pleasant faces!—whereas his face did nothing but blind everyone who looked at him. . . .

And when the queen went looking for her beloved son in the side room, she found him standing half-naked before the mirror and scrutinizing his diamond skin, his eyes dripping with bright tears.

"Darling son, my little crown, why are you crying? Why are you looking at your beautiful body that way?" the queen asked, and gathered him to her breast, alarmed. But the crown prince only wept even harder.

"Go away! You're making fun of me, too, Mama! Just

look at me," he wept bitterly. "Look at my face! Why do all the other children in the garden have such soft skin, yet my skin is so ugly?" And the crown prince sobbed so hard that his entire body shook as if with a fever.

From across the palace, the king heard his son weeping. He came running, frightened. And there he stood, a great ruler who could make millions of fathers happy or unhappy with a single decree—yet he did not know how to comfort his precious only son. He was prepared to give up treasuries full of riches if only it would make his son happy again. But happiness cannot be bought, even for all the riches in the world, and neither can you buy new flesh for your skin.

While the king and queen were still standing over their child with aching hearts, the door of the room suddenly slid open. A small red gnome with slender feet leapt lightly inside, bowing down to the ground before the king and queen and speaking to them in a voice that rang out like a bell:

"I've caught wind of your anguish and have come to help you." He whispered into the king's ear: "Bathe the crown prince in the tears of needy children, and his diamond skin will turn into ordinary soft skin."

And he bowed down again before the king and queen and vanished from the hall.

"It shall be done!" cried out the king, who, as a fearsome giant, was used to having his way. And he smiled with satisfaction.

A few hours later, the crown prince heard the terrible sound of weeping children coming from a faraway room in the palace. Curious, he ran to see. And to his surprise, he saw many little children assembled, some crippled and suffering terribly, others sickly with waxy, thin yellow faces, and still others swollen with hunger or crawling on their hands and knees. There were infants who'd been torn from their mothers' breasts. Many of the children were half-naked, and others were wrapped in rags. And all the children wept frightfully, and their hot tears ran, drop by drop, into golden basins that had been set out for that purpose.

"Why are these children crying, and why are their tears being collected in basins?" the crown prince asked, his heart quivering with horror.

"My little son, we're collecting their tears for a bath for you," the king explained proudly, stroking the boy's locks. "As soon as you bathe in these tears, you'll receive the soft, fleshly skin that you long for so dearly."

"No! No! No!" the crown prince shrieked, stamping his little foot, his whole body trembling. "I don't want to bathe in these children's tears! I don't want to!" And he stared at the children and said, "It's a pity they have to walk around in rags—and they must no doubt be hungry. Papa, see to it that they're cared for, with food and clothing, so they'll stop crying—and I'll just keep my face!"

The stern king had no choice but to obey his precious only son's wishes. But when the good-hearted crown prince woke up in his golden bed the next morning and opened his bright eyes in the streaming sunlight, he saw to his great joy and astonishment that his diamond skin had changed into ordinary soft skin of flesh, skin even more beautiful than that of the courtiers' children he had seen yesterday in the garden.

Translated by Ri J. Turner and David Stromberg

JUSTICE

THE BIRD CATCHER

Jacob Kreplak

It's summertime, and Shoyelke refuses to stay indoors for even a minute. As soon as he can, he slinks away from home and holes up in the garden so that no one can find him.

At home, it's boring—his father is busy with work, and his mother, as soon as she catches sight of him, always scolds him for being a complete loafer. "Most boys like you are already studying the Talmud." And, worst of all, he could be sent on an errand.

He hates errands. He can't stand being told what to do. In the garden, he's free, he does what he wants. He lies for hours in the cool grass, which has grown very thick among the trees by the tall fence. He blends in with the bird-meal and madman's poppy, and gets caught in the burrs, which will be thrown on the Ninth of Av.

When he's alone—when he doesn't see Esterke, the

neighbor's daughter, who also always plays in their garden—he hides himself in the grass and, through the blades, watches the colorful spotted ladybugs crawl higher and higher up the stalks, come to the top, and stop as if it were the end of the world. He picks up a stalk and pokes at them until they open a pair of wings and fly off—or fall down as if dead.

Hearing a cricket, he creeps up quietly, looks into its green eyes for a while, then grabs it by both legs and plays cat and mouse with it. He holds it in his fist and opens his hand so that it can leap out, while keeping the other hand ready to grab it.

If the cricket manages to escape, he follows its every leap—he lies low and hops up, as if riding on green waves—and grabs it, pulling off its saw-like leg. "Go, little cripple, let's see how you chirp now."

Feeling tired, he stretches out to see if there are any birds flying in the sky. He could catch all the birds. And in the clouds, he also sees rivers, mountains, and big, strange crickets.

In the evening, he chases swallows. It's a *mitzvah*—a good deed—to twist off their heads, because they carried fire to the Jerusalem Temple. It's not for nothing that their throats bear a red mark, while they themselves are scorched black.

When Esterke's in the garden, he plays with her by hiding in the grass and suddenly jumping out to scare her. The different creatures that Shoyelke holds scare her, and when he comes toward her with a cricket or a bee, she screams, watches him with frightened eyes, and hides her hands behind her back.

But she follows Shoyelke like a sheep and watches everything he does.

Esterke is now standing and watching Shoyelke put together five bricks to make a bird trap.

"I'll catch as many birds as you want," he boasts to her as he quickly makes a box out of four bricks, props up the top brick with a small piece of wood, places a little board under it, and scatters some crumbs of challah bread.

"Now let's hide." He pulls Esterke away to the side.

A host of sparrows descends, chirping like children, and scatters all over the trap. A group of younglings starts hopping on and around the bricks.

An elderly sparrow, a dignified uncle, stays at a distance, looking askance at the young twosomes as if warning them: don't be so joyful, don't let yourselves be fooled.

But the twosomes hop and peck, hop and peck.

Shoyelke and Esterke watch them.

"How many will you catch?" asks Esterke.

"A *he* and a *she*," replies Shoyelke.

"Will you give me any?"

"As many as you want."

"A *he* and a *she,* too."

"Sure."

"Shh." His eyes suddenly light up. "There's one coming. . . ."

"A *he* or a *she*?" asks Esterke.

"A *he.*"

"How do you know?"

"I know. He has a crown on his head," replies Shoyelke.

"I don't see it," returns Esterke.

"You can't see the crown," replies Shoyelke authoritatively. "Look! Look . . ."

He doesn't have time to finish the sentence before the top brick—zap!—drops with a clap.

A pitiful squeak—like a small child squealing with sudden pain—cuts through the air and dies out.

The entire host of sparrows rises up noisily and flies away. Shoyelke dashes out of his hideout while Esterke stays behind, frightened by the clapping sound.

"Two! Two in one go!" he shouts to her in joyful excitement. "Come here, you'll see—a *he* and a *she*!"

Like a professional, he uses his jacket to cover the bricks, and he sees that sticking out from one side is half a bird, crushed by the brick. The sparrow doesn't move, except for one open eye with a red stripe around it, which keeps blinking at him as if trying in vain to cry.

"What's wrong with the birdie?" Esterke comes up.

"It died," replies Shoyelke indifferently.

"You're no good at catching them." Esterke pouts her lips. "Poor birdie."

"No big deal, I can catch as many as you want. You've got *one,* anyway!"

He stretches out on the ground, peeps into a crack in the bricks, and sees a sparrow sitting hunched up, its feathers raised with fright.

"Want to see how our guest sits there?" Shoyelke gets up.

"I'm afraid of the dead one." Esterke looks fearfully on. "It could appear in a dream, like Grandma says."

Shoyelke laughs.

"You're such a granny!" he says with the same face his father makes when he says it to his mother. "It's not a person. It's just a bird. . . ."

• • •

In his sleep, Shoyelke feels someone pecking him ever so
lightly, as if with a tiny beak. He pinches himself and in
the dark sees a tiny open eye with a red stripe around it,
blinking at him as if trying in vain to weep.

He immediately remembers Esterke's words. The bird
has come to him in a dream, and, frightened, he wants to
shout, "Mama!" But the darkness around the eye starts to
brighten, and he sees a whole bird looking at him ever so
kindly. He seems to know this bird. "Why, it's Esterke!"
he marvels. "I'd swear it's Esterke, but she looks kind of
strange—like a real sparrow, with feathers, a pretty little
tail, trim little wings, a mouth like a tiny beak."

His heart rises. He can't contain himself any longer
and bursts out laughing.

"Esterke, why are you pretending to be a bird?"

"Why 'pretending'?" chirps Esterke so strangely, lov-
ingly rubbing her beak against him. "You're also a bird."

"I am?"

"Yes!"

He takes a look—it's true, he's also a sparrow, a real
he. He wants to stretch out a hand, to feel whether he has
a crown on his head, but it's not a hand he has at all, it's
a wing.

"Well, did I lie?" asks Esterke.

"I swear—it's true." Shoyelke no longer recognizes his voice, chirping like a bird. "Can we fly, too?"

"Of course!"

Shoyelke feels light and airy, as if he has no belly at all and is made up entirely of wings.

"Let's fly!"

"Let's."

Shoyelke takes off. "I swear I can fly!" He's still a little amazed.

Esterke flies after him. They circle around the room, and Shoyelke feels as if he could land on the hanging lamp, on the corner of the bookcase with the sacred books, anywhere he wants.

"Why are we flying around inside?" Shoyelke says to her. "We could wake up Mama and Papa. Let's fly away outside."

"Let's."

"Through where?"

"Where I came in—through the broken window-pane."

"Where shall we fly, to our garden or to Auntie's on the square?"

"Wherever you want."

"Let's fly far, far away."

"Let's fly."

Shoyelke ascends into the sky, flies around in circles, flies over the shingled roofs of their town, over the church spire, and dashes over the field. He looks down and sees their rivulet winding below like a ribbon and the curly treetops swaying.

A flock of pigeons, like a colored cloud, appears in the sky. Shoyelke feels like competing with them in speed, so he darts through them like a flung pebble and asks Esterke proudly:

"Who's faster?"

Esterke doesn't answer him but instead lets out a desperate shriek, and he sees a sparrow hawk hovering in the sky as if deciding on whom to strike—them or the pigeons.

"Faster, Esterke!" he shouts with all his might. "Fly! He's coming at us."

Esterke doesn't respond, and they pull up and down, up and down, swerve to the right, and dart to the left, with the sparrow hawk still in hot pursuit.

As far as the eye can see, Shoyelke sees the open sky and the flat earth, but something's looming on the horizon.

"Fly! Fly!" he keeps shouting to Esterke.

Esterke doesn't respond, but he feels her panic.

"Fly! Fly!" he keeps pressing her. "A little more and we'll be in the forest."

The sparrow hawk swoops down like the wind. They dart to one side, he follows, they dart back. This way, they fly around until they duck into the forest and huddle up under the branches, where the sparrow hawk can't get at them.

"Esterke! There's nothing to fear anymore," says Shoyelke as he watches Esterke cling to him.

"I'm tired and hungry," complains Esterke.

"We'll go down to the ground and find something," Shoyelke assures her.

"Let's."

No sooner said than done. Shoyelke and Esterke hop down and peck, forage with their beaks—no, nothing but bare moss and rotting mushrooms all around.

"I'm faint with hunger." Esterke suddenly bursts into tears.

"We'll have to fly home," Shoyelke says.

"Is home far?" asks Esterke.

"I don't know. I'll ask a chirper—he'll tell me."

Shoyelke finds a cricket.

"Where's my home?" he asks.

"Who are you?" asks the cricket, and watches him with his green eyes.

"I'm Shoyelke."

"Oh, Shoyelke the Leg Puller. I won't tell you."

Shoyelke dashes forward to peck at him, but the cricket leaps to one side and chirps with laughter: "Shoyelke the Leg Puller will die of hunger here."

"I'm starving," says Esterke, sobbing.

"I won't pull any more legs! Tell me!" cries Shoyelke.

"You swear?" The cricket stops laughing.

"I swear."

"Fly out of the forest, turn right, then left, and you'll be in your garden."

"Really?"

"Of course!"

"And I thought we were so far away!"

"That's because the sparrow hawk chased you around in circles," chirps the chirper.

"Farewell!"

"Keep your word!"

Shoyelke looks down, and indeed, the garden's just below! And here are the bricks, still arranged with crumbs of challah bread all around.

"Let's go down into the garden," suggests Shoyelke.

"Let's."

"I'm starving." Esterke looks at the scattered crumbs greedily. "What do you think, can I eat the challah?"

"You can—it's pure challah, I swear, I scattered it my-self," Shoyelke assures her. "What do we care, anyway? We're birds!"

And they hop over the bricks and peck with their beaks when suddenly—zap!—the top brick drops.

A pitiful squeak cuts through the air. Shoyelke sits on the bricks, his feathers raised in fear. Esterke lies crushed, and one eye keeps blinking as if trying in vain to weep.

Shoyelke wakes up in terror.

Translated by Lena Watson

THE PAPER KITE

Leon Elbe

A little boy made a paper kite and went up to his roof to let it fly.

The kite flew through the air, flying and floating and showing off its tricks, with a twist here and a turn there and a wag of its tail as if its tail were real—a tail like a snake. But the truth is that the tail was actually just a long, thin rag attached to the kite, which the boy had torn from an old apron that his mother no longer needed.

But what did it matter what the tail was made of? It was a tail. For a paper kite, it was a good tail—there was no need for a better one. The boy thought so, too, and he looked at the tail trailing behind the paper kite and beamed with joy.

The paper kite flew through the air, and it thought it could fly as high and as far as it wanted. The kite completely forgot that it also depended entirely on the wind, and that should the wind stop blowing, the kite, too, would have to stop flying. Aside from that, the boy was holding the kite on a string, and if he wanted to, he could pull the string toward himself, and that would be the end of its flight!

But the string was long enough for the kite to fly high and far without realizing from the outset that it was in the boy's hands. The kite flew off and tried hard to fly together with all the birds. All the birds looked at the kite and wondered: "What type of bird is this, and where does it come from?" They'd noticed many similar ones before, but this time they had to ask.

The birds asked the kite. It told them that it was not a bird but a kite—with a snaky tail. The birds were even more amazed. "A flying snake?" They'd heard of snakes, but snakes crawled around the ground, they didn't fly in the air. "A snake that can fly?" And the birds were frightened—because they'd heard that snakes had a kind of venom with which they can kill—and so they quickly turned from the kite and made off. When the paper kite noticed that the birds were fleeing, it thought even more highly of itself and puffed up. "Aha," it thought, "the birds are scared of me! I'll have to chase after them and catch a few!"

It darted after them with all its might. It forgot entirely that it was no more than a paper kite and that a boy was holding it by a string. It wanted to chase after the birds but couldn't. It thought: "What's the problem here?" It looked down and saw that the boy was holding it by a string. It wanted to tear free from the boy's hands but couldn't. It began to pull furiously, but to no avail. The boy laughed at it and said: "Don't pull like that, you paper golem. You'll tear yourself apart."

The paper kite said to the boy: "Let me off the string for a while, and I'll bring you back a little bird."

The boy laughed at it again and said: "How can you bring me a bird?"

The paper kite answered: "I flew with the birds and told them I was a kite with a snaky tail, and they were scared and flew away from me. Now I want to chase them and catch a couple. I'll give you one and keep one for myself."

The boy said to the paper kite: "Fine. I'll let you loose. Go and bring me a bird. But remember: don't fly too far and don't take too long."

The paper kite flew off just when the wind was quite strong. It flew high and far, and all the birds saw it flying fast, twisting its tail, so they were frightened of it

again and said to one another: "Beware, beware, a flying snake!"

An old bird heard this talk and said: "Why are you
running around like a bunch of crazies? What kind of
snake? I'm a pretty old bird by now, and I've never heard
of a flying snake. Maybe you mean a hot-air balloon or
an airplane?"

The birds all answered as one: "No, a snake with a
long tail."

The old bird said to them: "You don't say! Well then,
show me this snake. Let's have a look at it."

Just then, the wind carried the paper kite over, and
the frightened birds pointed it out. But the old bird burst
into laughter.

"This is the snake you're talking about?" it asked
them. "This here is the paper golem that scared you?
Bah! You fools! Just let me go right up to it and peck and
tear it apart with my old beak, and there'll be nothing
left of your paper hero."

The old bird flew toward the paper kite. The paper
kite puffed up even more and, seeing the old bird fly
toward it, exclaimed with joy: "Here, I've got one bird
already!"

But its joy didn't last long. The old bird sank its beak

and talons into the kite and tore it to tiny little shreds. When the young birds saw this, they clapped *bravo* with their wings. The old bird said to them: "Well, do you see now what kind of snake this is? It's just a paper kite! I saw with my own eyes how a boy once made such a paper kite. Now you'll know that you don't have to fear everything you see."

The birds flew off happily and merrily, but the paper kite could not, obviously, fly anymore. Torn and tattered, it fell down to the ground in a clearing, since finding its way back to the roof where the boy stood and waited for it was no longer possible.

The boy waited and waited. When he realized the kite wasn't coming back, he climbed off the roof and went looking for it until he found it, shredded and tattered, lying in a clearing. The boy could barely recognize it. He picked it up, took it home, and repaired it. Later, the boy stood on his roof again and let his paper kite fly. The paper kite did not pick any more fights with anyone, and it flew only as far as the boy would let it fly. It never flew any farther.

Translated by Sandra Chiritescu

TWO SISTERS

Jacob Reisfeder

Once upon a time, there were two sisters—two beautiful, good, happy sisters—who loved each other as much as they loved life itself.

When their mama and papa used to go into the fields at daybreak, these two sisters would lie in bed a little longer, hugging each other, playing around, and singing along with the little birds outside their window. This they did until seven o'clock, when they jumped up, got dressed, and ran out to wash up at the clear stream that flowed merrily past their house. Then one of them collected dry twigs, and the other started a fire. Once they finished preparing breakfast, they hugged each other again, and one of the sisters would run into the fields to bring food to Mama and Papa, while the other set herself to the task of cleaning the house, singing all the while. And by the time the first sister made her way back from the fields, the house was already shiny clean. Both sisters were extremely pleased to see their little house looking so nice, and they began to laugh and sing with joy. The little birds outside the window sang along with them, and the golden sun looked glowingly into the house to watch the two loyal sisters hugging each other.

They would pass the whole day this very same way, singing as they washed clothes at the river and frolicking as they prepared lunch. And when there were no chores left, they played in front of the house in the golden sunlight, and their sweet singing echoed through the wide fields for miles around.

In this way, they passed the time that remained until the sun began to set and Mama and Papa returned from the fields, bringing with them the fragrance of freshly mown hay. Then the two sisters ate supper with their parents and happily lay down in their bed, where they amused each other quietly for a long while until at last they dropped off to sleep.

This way, the sisters enjoyed each other's company day and night.

One day around midsummer, a rich woman from a nearby city arrived in the village with her son—a little boy with big blue eyes and beautiful blond locks. The rich woman had come to spend the summer in the

countryside, and rented a room from a peasant oppo-
site the house where the two sisters lived. The very next
morning, the little boy—already feeling quite at home
in the strange new place—played outside in the golden
sun, happily riding his leather horsey and cracking his
snappy whip, crying out, "Giddyup!" as his laughter
rang out like a bell.

The two sisters, hearing his sweet peals of laughter,
came out of their house. They stood on the porch, looking curiously at the lovely, merry little boy in his white
pants and brown sandals. Never before had they seen
such a golden boy. They were used to the sight of the
barefoot peasant children.

They came down from the stoop and approached the
little boy tentatively. When he saw them, he fell silent
and stopped cracking his whip over the horsey's back.

The children looked shyly at one another for a long
moment.

The little boy was the first to speak, his eyes flashing:
"Come on, girls, let's play together. Here's the whip. You
want it? Or maybe the ball? Wait until you see how far I
can throw!"

The sisters wanted to play ball. Neither of them had
ever held a ball. The three beautiful children played together for a long while, their cheeks flaming, throwing

the big, soft ball to one another and laughing. But suddenly the sisters realized they had not yet cleaned the
house or prepared lunch.

For the first time in their lives, the two sisters began
to bargain with each other.

"You go inside and clean up," commanded the elder
sister without taking her eyes off the boy.

"I don't want to! You go! I'm too tired," grumbled her
little sister, refusing to budge from the little boy's side.

Both sisters very much wanted to continue playing
with him.

"Go, I said!" cried the elder sister with fiery eyes.

"I said I don't want to, so you go!" her little sister
shouted in her face.

At that, the elder sister grabbed her by the hair, and
the younger sister started scratching at her big sister's
face. But the elder was stronger, and the younger was
forced to run away, sobbing out loud from the shame.
Yet instead of going inside to clean up, she ran down to
the riverbank.

She stood by the clear silvery waters of the stream
and wept bitterly over her sister's making a fool of her in
front of the little boy.

Just then, a golden fish swam to the riverbank and
looked at her, its shiny eyes full of pity.

"Little girl, little girl, why do you cry so? Who's hurt you?" The little girl pulled back, frightened to hear the fish speaking to her just like a person. "I'm the little fish to whom you used to throw bread crumbs every day while playing by the riverside. Tell me who hurt you, and I'll avenge you."

"My sister!" the little girl sobbed. "She drove me away from the little boy, and now she has him all to herself!"

"Hush. I'll take revenge on her for you," the little fish told her. "You'll soon be the one playing with the little boy."

And the little fish splashed with its golden tail and disappeared deep into the water. But suddenly the little girl was seized with terror about the fish's revenge on her sister, and Mama and Papa's reaction.

So she raced into the house to do her chores, and resolved to save her sister from the fish's revenge. After all, they were still sisters! And she burst out crying again, but this time out of pity for her sister.

The next morning, when the elder sister went to bathe in the river, her little sister jumped up and ran over to stand in her way.

"Don't go! The little fish is going to hurt you! Oh, don't go!" she begged her.

But the elder sister refused to listen to her and ran down to the river to bathe.

Her frightened little sister tiptoed after her and hid by the riverbank near the place where her big sister was bathing in the clear water.

Suddenly the little golden fish swam over to her, leapt into the air, fastened its little teeth onto her beautiful long hair, and began to drag her down into the water. In another minute, she would drown! But her little sister jumped up from her hiding place with a frightful cry:

"Little fish! Little fish! Don't kill her! Take pity, don't drown my only sister! Mama and Papa will cry, and I'll cry, too, because I love my sister!"

The golden fish at once let go of the elder sister's hair and ashamedly disappeared into the water.

The two sisters embraced and clung to each other for a long time, and they swore an oath to love each other just as they had in the past, and never to fight about anything in the world ever again.

Translated by Ri J. Turner and David Stromberg

A FIGHT

Jacob Kreplak

A war broke out among the boys.

With copies of the *humash*, the five books of Moses, still under their arms, the younger classes played Mount Sinai in the evening, straight after school.

"Mount Sinai"—a long, flat slab, half-buried in the middle of the unpaved, sandy synagogue courtyard—was occupied and cleared by the boys.

"My Mount Sinai!"

"Get off! My Mount Sinai!"

They fought, pushing each other around like sparrows in the dusty sand, jostling and clambering onto the slab.

"I'm Moses!"

"No! I'm already standing here. I'm Moses!"

It was a golden summer evening. Somewhere far off, behind the roof of the tall synagogue, the flaming-red sun was setting with a glow. Above the boys' heads, the thin, dry dust, together with the noise, hung as if motionless in the air. Here and there, little clouds of rhythmic mosquitoes swarmed between heaven and earth. Beetles kept blindly bumping into the old walls of the synagogue in midflight and suddenly dropping down, without managing to fold their transparent lower wings.

As if out of nowhere, swallows darted swiftly from under the shingled roofs of the study houses and the tall roof of the synagogue, and flew every which way with a soft twitter, dropping to the very ground like flung pebbles and immediately shooting up to the sky as fast as arrows.

When one of the boys, throwing back his head, spotted a bat—fluttering in the air like a leaf torn off by the wind, and seeming itself not to know where to fly—he'd shout:

"Bring something white! Quick, something white, to get its attention!"

The youngest boys played buttons or just watched the sky, and as soon as they saw a flock of birds moving across the sky to their nightly stopover, they'd sing in chorus:

> *Quick, the house is burning . . . down.*
> *Throw a purse of money . . . down.*

Everything buzzed and hummed as if a taut string vibrated in the air the whole time. Yet the town's weary Jews hurried across the synagogue courtyard to evening prayers in the study houses, wiping sweat from their faces and paying no attention to the noise made by the children. Above them, dark stripes lay across the sky like wrinkles, giving it a pensive late-afternoon appearance.

Near Mount Sinai, amid the commotion, a piercingly shrill little voice was almost crying.

"Ow-ow-ow! My pant leg! My pants! Blabbermouth, why are you pulling at me? You're tearing my pant leg, you're tearing it!"

Tsalkele Blabbermouth, a puffed-up boy bloated like a bladder, had latched on to Yankele's foot, pushing himself against the stone and dragging Yankele off Mount Sinai with all his might.

"Blabbermouth, you'd better let go," threatened the little voice.

"No, Questionhead, I won't. You're calling names!"

Yankele Questionhead, splayed flat on his tummy, was holding his *humash* high in one hand, and with the other was clutching at the stone. He yelled again that his pant leg was tearing and, feeling he'd be dragged down any minute, tried to hold on with both hands, forgetting about the *humash* and letting it go.

"The *humash*! The *humash* is falling!" shouted Yankele Questionhead in fear, and at once saw the *humash* open its covers as a bird opens a pair of wings, flipping over the stone and falling in the sand.

"Blabbermouth, let go! Careful, don't step on it!" the boys began to shout, all scrambling to pick up the *humash*.

"I picked it up first. I get to kiss it!" said one boy, out of breath.

"What are you talking about? You need to kiss the spot where it fell," interrupted a boy with prickly eyes and freckles.

"Get lost, you red-headed Roman. You don't know a thing—Questionhead has to kiss it," butted in a scruffy-looking boy who hadn't heard what was said. "It was Questionhead who dropped it."

"Blabbermouth, too!" the others chimed in. "They're both guilty. They both have to kiss it," the other boys said, passing their ruling.

Without the *humash*, Yankele Questionhead now had a better grip on the stone and squealed shrilly:

"Blabber! Blabbermouth! The sin is on your head. Let go!"

But Tsalkele Blabbermouth—his face puffed up and

red—stubbornly and dumbly, like an ox, still wouldn't let go of him.

"Blabbermouth, let go!" The others pounced on him. "We'll punch you in the sides. . . ."

Feeling he'd been freed, Yankele Questionhead jumped off the stone in agitation, losing his cap, and ran at Tsalkele Blabbermouth, fixing him with his black eyes and starting to hit himself in the chest, swearing like a grown-up:

"As true as I'm a Jew, I'll kill you!"

"Kiss the *humash*." A boy brought him his *humash*.

"Some trick! To drag me down by the foot—that's his trick, that Blabbermouth." Yankele was boiling. "I dropped the *humash* because of him."

Tsalkele turned even redder. Having sensed that the boys weren't on his side, he sulked and grumbled:

"Why are you calling names, huh?"

"I'll show you *calling names*." Yankele felt he was in the right. "Blabbermouth!"

"Questionhead!"

"Why are you calling names, huh?" Yankele flared up and started all over again. "You think I'll be quiet? You think I'm afraid of *you*?" Yankele moved closer to Blabbermouth's face, sensing that the boys admired him and getting even more excited. "You think I'm afraid of you because you're a head taller? I'll go one-on-one with you."

The boys' eyes lit up.

"One-on-one," many of them echoed. "Question-head's right. Make a circle."

The boys made a circle.

"Come on, take a poke." Yankele Questionhead stood sideways like a hero as he watched Tsalkele Blabber-mouth with vigilant eyes.

"*You* . . . take a poke first!" Tsalkele Blabbermouth let the words roll slowly off his tongue.

"Questionhead, you start!" the impatient ones egged on.

"Don't butt in. It's one-on-one," insisted the others.

"Here, I've touched you." Yankele touched Tsalkele's jacket with his finger.

Tsalkele was now red as a beet. He slowly turned his head and said stubbornly:

"That isn't touching."

"It is touching, it is!" the boys yelled.

Tsalkele Blabbermouth kept shaking his head and stood his ground.

"That isn't touching."

"Poke him harder!" the other boys incited Yankele.

"I know!" Yankele now felt like a big shot and gave a prod with his finger, a little harder.

"He touched you, he touched you, we saw it!" the boys started yelling again.

"Here, take it back."

Tsalkele saw he could no longer help it, and in the same way, slowly touched Yankele's jacket with his finger.

"Why are you hitting me?"

Yankele, pretending to cry, suddenly pounced on Tsalkele. They grabbed each other and began rolling around in the sand, as if in soft eiderdown, stirring up a cloud of dust.

The other boys bent over them and followed them intently, stretching the circle according to how they rolled, supervising and warning them:

"The stone, you're rolling onto the stone! To the side, to the side!"

"My goodness, little urchins, why are you killing each other?" suddenly sounded the voice of Leah, the sexton's wife—a tall, withered woman with hairy warts on her face, whom they feared and who they were sure could do magic.

"Little bandits, why are you letting Jewish children fight? Wait till I tell your fathers!"

She grabbed Yankele and Tsalkele and lifted them from the sand.

Still heated from the fight, at first they didn't see who had lifted them, and both blurted out at the same time:

"Well, who packed a better punch?"

But soon they broke free and ran to the other boys, who had scattered across the synagogue courtyard.

"Here are your caps." The other boys handed them their caps with particular friendliness.

"Here, I'll brush you off from behind," others offered helpfully.

"Don't forget to kiss the *humash,* both of you," the boy with the freckles reminded them.

Stars spilled out across the sandy sky. A while later, the fathers spilled out of the study houses, and the boys went home.

Translated by Lena Watson

THE BROKEN MIRROR

Moyshe Nadir

There once were identical twin brothers—one older than the other by just a few minutes.

From their parents, they inherited a mirror. What kind of mirror, you ask? Not a hand mirror, and not a round hanging mirror like those in some houses nowadays, but a standing mirror—old-fashioned, long, taller than a person—one of those rare polished mirrors we see only in royal courts and in stone castles in Spain or France.

From the palace that the parents left after their deaths, the brothers slowly sold off the fancy furniture, the original paintings, the porcelain plates, and the rare tapestries, curtains, rugs, and ivory pieces. Because aside from a big chunk of real estate, the brothers had also inherited some bad blood—blue blood, their parents had called it. The parents were even proud of it, and this in itself was enough to show the kinds of brains they had, not knowing that healthy people's blood is red and not blue! In short, the twin brothers—who were named Anik and Manik—had drunk away, squandered, and wasted the entire estate. They first ate up the gold goblets and the silver spoons and then started on a diet of pearls and ivory. They would regularly, each day, eat three big, glimmering green pearls and for dessert have a Chinese figurine of rose ivory. That is, they didn't actually eat the pearls and ivory, but bought food and drink after selling them. And they wore wooden clothes—that is, pants, vests, jackets, and overcoats acquired with money from the last pieces of fine furniture that they sold.

They were left with the rare grand mirror—which they set aside for the very end. First of all, because it was unique and expensive, and they didn't want to part with it until they found the right buyer. Second of all, the twin brothers, Anik and Manik, were extremely vain, and these self-loving peacocks enjoyed standing for minutes at a time in front of the mirror, grimacing, flirting with themselves, sticking out their tongues, making all kinds of silly faces. . . .

Then this happened: Anik, the younger of the two (only five minutes younger!), made a clumsy move with his cane, and knak, kerplunk! The mirror broke into bits and pieces. In the corners of the frame were triangular shards of glass, which were also split into pieces—like ripples on a river.

When Anik saw what he'd managed to do, he became red, and then pale, and his heart started banging like a clock. He thought there was only one thing left for him to do: to take the dagger—which lay sideways in a Chinese ivory sheath—down from the wall and stick the blade into his heart.

"And . . . and . . . and . . . and . . ."

But no. He thought it over. Then a happier thought occurred to him: he himself would stand in the frame, and when his older brother, Manik, came home, Anik would mirror him—that is, whatever the other did, he would do, too, so that his brother wouldn't catch on that there was no glass in the mirror.

One hour, two hours, three . . . A-ring, ting-ting-ting, went the old doorbell. The older brother, Manik—dressed, as usual, in his black overcoat, and holding a cane—came into the palace hall, a little drunk, as always. He was in high spirits. He put the cane away in a corner, hung his hat on the rack, and pulled first one white glove off his hand and then the other, looking at himself in the mirror while pulling off the second glove.

The younger brother, Anik, mimicked exactly what

the other did, carefully pulling off a glove. When Manik opened his mouth and scratched his head, yawning deeply and heavily, Anik did the same thing. When Manik felt his long, horsey face to see whether it was time to shave, Anik made the same gestures. And when Manik started carefully bending his knees up and down, doing his usual bedtime exercises, Anik did the same— just as if he were not a person but a mirror.

This went on for a good ten minutes. By that time, Manik had undressed all the way to his pants and further looked at himself in the mirror: at the lowered chest and pale arms, from which his hands and fingers hung down like rags. Anik was not bad at mirroring him, since in all these things, he and his brother were like two drops of water.

It was all going excellently, and Anik was about to be pleased with his success—when suddenly! The self-indulgent Manik, today even more than usual, especially liked the way he looked in the mirror. And since he was a little drunk and feeling good, he decided to flick his own nose in the mirror. Anik had no choice but to flick him back. Manik was astonished: until now, it had never happened to him that his reflection in the mirror could . . . flick him back on the nose. The whole thing made him very upset. He took a couple of steps back from the mirror, raised his finger, and said: "Hey, crazy Manik"—he meant himself—"you should cut out your little act, or I'll give you a good punch!" He then put his fist straight into Anik's eye, and, obviously, Anik had to respond in kind.

Manik was now even more angry. He rushed over to the table, poured himself a big glass of whiskey, gulped it down, and wanted to roll up his sleeves. But he was already half-undressed—without a shirt, so he just stood there, with sweaty, disheveled hair, and, with mouth frothing, looking stubbornly and childishly at the floor, thinking about what he should do. Then he suddenly rolled up his pants and grabbed a bottle from a pile of empty ones standing next to the mirror. Anik did the same, and—hack, knak, boom—they started hitting each other on the head until they both fell, bloody all over. Manik, with a bottle in his hand, was still whispering: "You nasty me, you! . . . You hit yourself with bottles, no less, you drunkard. You ne'er-do-well, you good-for-nothing. . . ."

When a certain poor neighbor came by in the morning to ask them what time it was—they'd always tell him, free of charge, merely in exchange for his cleaning out their stables once a week and brushing their two horses—he found the two brothers lying on the cold floor, in a river of broken mirror glass. They were both in nearly the exact same position, with bottles in their hands. It was as if a man had fought his own shadow, and both of them had won. . . .

Translated by David Stromberg

WONDER

A SQUIRREL'S DIARY

Sonya Kantor

EARLY SPRING

It's so exciting to finally be able to jump up and down the green branches of our tree, to crack nuts, and to chase big worms and flies—all by myself!

I remember, as if in a dream, that just a short while ago I was weak and helpless.

Not for a second did Mama leave me or my younger sister, Libele. Papa brought us nuts, cracked them himself, and put the sweet kernels into our mouths. How long ago was that?

And now I feel like I could jump across the whole world!

Libele is weaker than I am. She's still sitting in the nest. But I can't stay put in the nest any longer. The sun's shining! The birds are singing! It's so fun, so exciting, all around. I'd like to jump through all the trees, but Mama has warned me not to go too far from the nest.

I have to describe my whole family to you. Mama and Papa love us very much. When we were still tiny, Mama licked us clean and brushed us with her paws. "Look, dear, what beautiful children we have. The world hasn't seen more beautiful squirrels than ours," she often used to say to Papa.

Papa looks at us proudly. He teaches us to run across the smooth tree trunk, to hop from the trunk to the nearest branches, to jump from one tree to another. He teaches us how to catch worms, how to hold a nut, how to crack it open, and how to spit out the shell.

We live in a big park, in the hollow of a tall old tree. Mama and Papa built a warm nest on the uppermost branches. We have a soft bed made of leaves, twigs, and moss. Above us is a canopy. It protects us from rain and wind. When the sun's out, I love dancing all around on the trees. Mama and Papa don't let us hop too far by ourselves. "You're still young and not careful. You could be snatched away by a weasel or an owl."

I don't understand how I could be snatched away by anyone. I've already seen an owl once—it's a blind old bird. Before it even stirs, I'll run off far, far away!

I haven't seen a weasel yet. Papa says weasels can jump as fast as we can, but I don't believe it. I think he's only scaring us. He just doesn't want us to run far away.

EARLY SUMMER

Yesterday Papa and Mama went to visit friends. Libele and I stayed at home by ourselves.

"My son," said Papa, "keep an eye on your sister. She's still frail. Don't fight with her. You have a couple of nuts and acorns here. If it's not enough for you, you can pick a few from the tree yourself. Just remember, my child, don't go far. Be careful!"

Papa and Mama went away. We were left alone.

The sun shone and cast broad shadows across the park's long pathways. I couldn't stop jumping and dancing all over the tree branches.

Tap-tap, tap-tap. I heard an unfamiliar knocking.

"Libele, who is it? Who's knocking like this?" I asked. Libele didn't reply.

"Come, Libele, let's jump. Let's see what's there."

"And what will Papa say? Don't go, Nutcracker. I'm scared."

But I was already off. I leapt, stopped, listened to where the sound was coming from, and jumped again from tree to tree. Suddenly I saw a narrow crack in a tree and heard a squeak.

Mama and Papa punish me all the time for my curiosity. Well, I'm very curious. I went up to the crack and stuck my nose inside. I couldn't see anything, but I heard the squeak again. I curved my back to make it as thin as I could and slipped inside the crack.

It was dark. I saw nothing. I went through a narrow passage and suddenly found myself in a huge nest. Five tiny baby birds sat huddled together.

Then I saw a big bird with a long beak, in which she carried worms for her babies.

I was afraid, but the bird even more so. She flew back a little. In one breath, I slipped out of the crevice and made off.

I ran on and on. The sun set. I looked around: I didn't know where to go. I was lost.

What would happen now? The park was large, and I was all alone. I looked around helplessly.

I stopped to catch my breath. With a fresh, cool gust of wind, my nose picked up a familiar smell. I set off again, in the direction of the scent. I ran, stopped, sniffed, and ran again until I spotted our sweet tree.

I was up in the nest in a flash!

"Where have you been?" exclaimed Mama, weeping with joy. "We've been crying our eyes out! . . . Why aren't you answering? *Where have you been?*"

"Let me rest a little. . . . I crawled into a woodpecker's

nest. . . . I saw five baby birds. . . . I ran away from their mother. . . . And I got lost!"

"No harm done," Papa said. "You take after me. You'll go far!"

"But please be careful next time, Nutcracker! We've been so anxious," said Mama tenderly. "Now go to bed!"

Tired but satisfied, I curled up in my little bed and went straight to sleep.

HOT SEASON

Every day, it gets hotter in the park. I'm strong now. So is Libele. We already know the whole park. Now Libele can also sneak into a bird's nest and suck out the eggs. What else is new? All the birds have a lot of respect for us.

A weasel has chased me more than once. He really is very fast, but I'm fast and smart—and he can't catch me.

I know all the animals in our park. Papa's pleased with me. He says that by next spring, I'll be able to build my own nest.

He also says that besides the animals, you have to be very careful with people. I haven't seen them yet.

"Humans," Papa says, "are stronger and smarter than all the animals."

Even more than weasels? It can't be.

THUNDERSTORM SEASON

What a thunderstorm we had in our park today! I haven't seen such flashes of lightning or heard such claps of thunder in my whole life.

Earlier it was hot and humid. I had no energy to jump, and it was hard to breathe. I looked around. Suddenly everything was still: the leaves didn't rustle, the wind didn't blow. A heavy black cloud covered the sun and the entire sky.

All the birds flew around, confused and frightened, looking for their nests.

A heavy rain fell, and suddenly the sky split in half and bright lightning cut right through the whole overcast sky. Soon afterward came the thunder. I hadn't heard such a clap in all my life.

"Are you coming inside?" Papa called from the nest.

We went inside and I hid in a corner. Everyone sat quietly without moving, like a mouse, though Libele was crying.

Then the trees began to groan, the leaves to fall, and

thunder followed lightning again and again, until suddenly a thunderbolt hit a tree that stood not far from us.

I shut my eyes tight against the mighty flash.

But the peals of thunder grew farther and farther apart. It got lighter little by little. The rain stopped and only dripped from the branches. The air smelled strongly of tree resin and grass.

I went outside slowly. Many big trees had been broken. The tree that had been hit by a thunderbolt had split in two and was still smoking.

"Where are you off to, silly?" Mama pulled me back in by the tail. "Wait until the sun shines. . . . Just look at the state of his fur."

I got back into the nest. Libele was still crying.

HUNTING SEASON

I saw people for the first time today. Papa's right. Humans are strong.

I was sitting on a branch high in a tree and cracking nuts. Libele was sitting on a branch beneath and doing the same.

"You know, Nutcracker, I'm cutting new teeth," she exclaimed with joy.

Her teeth have been ground down, since Libele

obviously has a really big sweet tooth. But she was afraid she'd no longer be able to crack nuts.

I was very happy and immediately jumped to the branch she was sitting on.

Suddenly we heard a rustle and heavy steps. We looked down through the branches, and I don't know why, but I felt really scared. I dropped all my nuts.

We had never seen animals like these in our wild old park.

They lifted something off their backs and pressed it against their shoulders. A short bang sounded, and a fiery spark struck the tree, not far from where we were sitting.

"Run, Libele!" I shouted, jumping from branch to branch.

When I told Mama everything, she said, "Those were people, our worst enemies." Now I understand why people are even stronger than weasels.

NUTS AND SEEDS

Summer's gone. I look at our park and can't recognize it. Nothing's green anymore. Between the branches, you see yellow, red, and brown. And so many hazelnuts, acorns, and beechnuts!

What a life it is for us now, what a joy! You can forage all you want—under every leaf, on every tree. If it isn't a nut, it's a pinecone. If it isn't a pinecone, it's an acorn. And if it's neither of those, it's a seed that the wind has scattered.

Papa says we need to feed less. It's better to save for the bitter winter, when even a seed is hard to come by.

I listen to him, but our Libele has such a sweet tooth! She doesn't want to understand at all. But yesterday she nearly paid for her sweet tooth with her life.

A cold rain had been falling nonstop for a couple of days. Then yesterday it turned warm, and the sun shone again.

We jumped from tree to tree, deeper and farther into our park. We found ourselves in a corner that was unfamiliar to us. Suddenly Libele called out to me:

"Look, Nutcracker, some nice-looking little people are sitting by the window in that small house. They're doing something and don't see us. I'd love to know what they're busy doing all day. I don't see them jumping around or cracking nuts like we do."

And with one leap, she got down from our tree and jumped onto a chestnut tree that stood near the window.

The children heard the rustle of the branches. They lifted their eyes and saw us, then started whispering something to each other. In a bit, the little girl brought sweet almonds, scattered them on the ground, and hid under a tree.

"Libele, don't go!" I said. "Remember—you'll be sorry!"

But Libele, as you know, has a very sweet tooth. She didn't hear me and jumped right down. I followed. Suddenly a hat dropped on us, and the girl had us. But I scratched and bit her finger so badly that she let go of her brother's hat and ran back home, crying.

"It's all because of you and your sweet tooth," I shouted when we were back in the tree.

"And you don't have a sweet tooth, then, do you? Why did you come along?"

I was ashamed to admit it was true.

"I was afraid for you," I explained.

"Of course, as if I don't know!"

We would've surely fought for a long time if not for Mama and Papa: they made peace between us.

BIRD MIGRATION

It's cold in the park. Winds blow, yellow leaves fall. All the birds flock together in large groups and fly away from us.

"Where are they going?" I asked Papa.

"They're cold here, my child. They're looking for warmth and light, so they're flying off to lands where it's always warm."

"What about us? Why aren't we running off to warmer lands?"

"We'll find a way to get through the hard times here."

Our uncle, who lives in the forest, has come to visit us today. Mama called us over.

"Dear children," she said, "the lovely summer is gone. Hard times are coming. There will no longer be any nuts or seeds. We must prepare well with stores of food for the entire winter so that we don't suffer hunger and hardship. Your uncle has suggested we move from here to the forest. It's bigger than our park. Your uncle has already found a warm, dry hollow for us. Now it's time for you to help us stock up on food. You need to feed less, and instead bring everything into our storeroom. Libele, stop fidgeting! Listen to what I'm telling you, you little glutton. If you eat too much now, you'll starve in the winter."

We promised Mama to help with the difficult preparations.

TOIL AND LABOR

Days of toil and hard work have started for us. We run back and forth all day, gathering acorns, pinecones, and nuts, and dragging them all over to different spots in the forest. I don't know how we'll remember where we put our stashes. Papa says we need to put them in different places—perhaps he knows better.

It's lots of fun in the forest. Our whole family lives here, and we've already made new friends, too.

SNOW

We finished preparing our food stores a couple of days ago. After that, we just lay curled up in our nest. We didn't even feel like running out of the nest. It didn't stop raining.

Yesterday it snowed for the first time. It snowed all day, and the ground and trees were all covered with white fluff.

I ran outside right away. The sun shone, reflecting in the snowflakes, which sparkled like diamonds.

I found my friends. I really like one of them. Libele is pretty, but my girlfriend is even prettier.

"A lovely couple," says my family about us when we jump around together, looking for seeds.

DEEP FROST

Powerful frosts have set in. The forest is still and white. It dreams its winter dreams, but we aren't bored. I love dancing on crackling branches, running on the ground, and watching my own tracks in the snow. Every now and then, a deer runs by. Sometimes a gray hare comes hopping along, stops, pricks up his long ears, and is off again. Sometimes a black raven comes flying. Even he has turned paler.

Yesterday people came to the forest. They were dressed warmly. They were wearing tall hats on their heads and gloves on their hands.

I'm not cold, either. For winter, I grew a new thick, dark coat.

I hid in the nest and peeked out.

They marked many young firs and pines and left.

Today they came back with axes and saws and chopped down the young firs and pines.

I feel sorry for the little young trees.

WINTER ENDS

We don't leave our nest for weeks at a time. We lie curled up and sleep all day long. Once in a while, when we're very hungry, we run out to our food stashes to get something to eat.

But I'm bored. My head has started to spin from all this whiteness. I yearn for the sun, for the young green grass, for hazelnuts and chestnuts.

WARM SUNLIGHT

I'm getting ready to move back to our old park. My girlfriend's coming with me. It's getting warmer every day. The snow melts, water drips from the trees. Flowers sprout, our creek is flowing. The birds arrive from the warm lands. The air resounds with their singing and warbling.

I'd also like to wander around the world, as they do. They say there are no squirrels in the warm lands. I asked a cuckoo.

"Cuckoo, cuckoo," he replied. "None, none!"

How is that possible?

BLOOMING AND REBIRTH

We've been in our sweet park for two weeks now. I know and love every path and corner here. The flowers have already bloomed. Bluebells, lilies, and violets fill the air in our park with fragrance. Golden bees land on every flower and suck out the nectar. The birds lay eggs in their nests. My nest is built on a tall tree, separate from our parents'. Libele also has a boyfriend. She lives not far from us. We see each other a couple of times a day.

But now I'm preoccupied and busy. I have no time to write in my diary, either. After all, I'm going to become a father soon!

And so I'm ending my diary.

Translated by Lena Watson

GUR ARYEH

Rachel Shabad

There was once, in Prague, a great rabbi whose name was Gur Aryeh. He was a virtuous person and a great sage, and people from surrounding cities, towns, and villages would come to him for advice and blessings.

His name reached the king of the land, and the king ordered for Gur Aryeh to be brought to the palace.

When the rabbi came to the king and the king realized Gur Aryeh was a great sage, he became dearer to the king than all his courtiers, and the king would constantly seek his advice.

The courtiers took a disliking to the rabbi and constantly looked for some trick with which to expel him from the king's palace.

Every month, the courtiers would host a dinner for the king. The king would come and revel with them all night. The fires in the palace would burn like golden suns, and the sweet sounds of violins would waft lightly through the bright palace windows.

Gur Aryeh was not wealthy, because he always distributed his money among the poor and oppressed. He never hosted any dinners for the king, and once he even said: "Better to give the money for those dinners to the poor."

Once the eldest courtier said to the king: "Your Majesty, the king! All your courtiers and officials constantly host lavish dinners in your honor, and you revel all night with them, but the rabbi who resides in your palace has never done so. He has never hosted a dinner for the king."

Upon hearing these words, the king called for the rabbi and said: "Listen, my friend! My courtiers say you do not admire me. My courtiers always host merry dinners for me, but you have never done so. It seems as if you actually did not admire me. . . ."

The rabbi answered: "Your Majesty, the king! In a week from now, I shall host a feast in your honor, and I will also invite your courtiers."

That same day, the king met his eldest courtier and told him what Gur Aryeh had said. The courtier burst into laughter and said: "Your Majesty, the king, don't believe him. You should know that he's very poor. His pockets are empty. How can he host a meal?"

The king shrugged and said: "The rabbi is a very honest man. He always does as he says."

Several days later, the courtiers secretly sent someone to see whether the rabbi was preparing for the feast. He returned quickly, his sides splitting with laughter. His eyes brimmed with tears, his open lips pressed against his teeth from laughter.

"Why are you laughing so hard? Tell us, what did you see there?" all the courtiers asked in one voice.

As his laughter subsided somewhat, he managed to mutter with difficulty: "The rabbi's sitting around and studying. His home is empty and dead . . . no trace of any feast."

The eyes of the eldest courtier began to twinkle. "Well, well," he said, "the little rabbi will have an unhappy ending. The king will surely chase him out of the palace."

Again, several days passed. Again, the courtiers sent a spy. They still weren't reassured: maybe the preparations for the rabbi's feast had already commenced? The spy went and returned and again laughed. "What can I tell you? Nothing's new. The rabbi's sitting around and studying. Apparently, he's entirely forgotten about the whole thing." The courtiers clapped their hands, stroked their handsome beards, and said with joy and pleasure:

"Good! He's sure to meet an unhappy end. Now the king will recognize that the little rabbi has fooled him. . . ."

The day of the feast quickly approached. Impatient, the courtiers could hardly sleep the night before. They couldn't close an eye. They wanted to see revenge taken against the rabbi who was so liked by the king. As soon as day broke, they jumped out of their beds, dressed themselves, and ran to see what was happening with the feast.

Meanwhile, time was running out. Now there was only an hour left until the feast—and the rabbi was not here yet. Now there was only half an hour until the feast—and it was as quiet everywhere as in a graveyard. There was no work, no meal being prepared.

"Of course he won't come," they said quietly among themselves as their eyes shone with glee.

At that very moment, the rabbi appeared, dressed in his finest attire, and invited the king and courtiers to the feast. The courtiers looked at one another and didn't utter a word.

Soon thereafter, they sat down in beautiful chariots and drove out of the city, together with the rabbi, while the king drove ahead. They traveled and traveled and suddenly saw a beautiful palace with a garden around it. In the garden, there were huge trees with golden fruit hanging from their branches. The rabbi stopped the chariots and invited the king and all his guests into the palace.

As soon as they entered the palace, young slender servants with white towels on their shoulders emerged from tall open doors. Again the courtiers looked at one another, and though their faces burned with rage and shame, they were silent and didn't say a word.

Suddenly another tall door opened, and the guests beheld a large room with long golden tables and golden chairs. On the golden tables were all kinds of good things to eat, and the golden platters holding the food glowed like fire. Between the plates and glasses, there were wreaths of pearls, and loose diamonds, and other jewels. A blue light emanated from the walls as if from the sky.

"How beautiful and good it is here," the king thought, but he didn't say anything.

"My honorable guests!" the rabbi called out. "Take a seat at the table, and enjoy the food and drink."

The king sat down at the table, and all his courtiers sat around him. A servant soon stood behind every chair and waited for each guest's smallest command.

The guests first conversed with one another, and then they ate. A good light wine that didn't make the guests drunk was poured from crystal carafes into tall glasses. They all felt that they'd never seen such a beautiful and luxurious feast.

Neither was music lacking. From time to time, they heard an orchestra playing music, yet they couldn't see it. Here, too, delightful sounds wafted lightly through the bright windows.

The king, who was used to golden palaces and bejeweled plates, had never in his life seen such opulence and splendor. The saltshaker seemed a mere trifle—yet he had never in his life seen such a beautiful one. This saltshaker was decorated with diamonds and sparkled with green-and-red glimmer.

The feast lasted many hours, and eventually the guests went out into the garden. The slender trees lit by the sun stood proudly and silently. But their branches, heavily laden with ripe fruit, bowed down to the guests and urged them: "Enjoy my fruit . . . enjoy my fruit. . . ."

It was easy to pluck the fruit from the trees, and they melted on the tongue like sugar.

The king tasted the fruit, walked along the smooth, tree-lined paths—shining as if covered in gold—and stared. Everything here was new and as beautiful as it could only be in a dream, but the king uttered not a single word.

The sun was flaming red behind the gigantic trees, and it was getting late. Happy and grateful, the king looked at the garden one last time and prepared to travel home. The courtiers gathered around him, and slowly they strolled out of the garden.

But the eldest courtier couldn't move from where he sat—as if he were chained to the ground.

Another courtier asked him: "Why are you sitting down? Come with us!"

The eldest courtier answered with a pained face: "I can't get up."

The other courtier stepped closer, bent down, and asked: "Who's holding you back? There's no one here!"

But the eldest courtier yelled in a choked voice: "Help! I can't get up! Help! What's happened to me?"

The other courtier said: "Try, maybe you can get up. . . ."

He tried with all his might but couldn't. His feet wouldn't budge, as if they were tied down. And his eyes, filled with raging anger, seemed to want to burst out from under his wrinkled forehead. He yelled curses at the rabbi with his palace and his feast.

The other courtier ran to the king and related everything to him. The king was stunned and went to look at what had happened to his eldest courtier.

He reached the spot and saw the courtier sitting as if he were chained to the ground, his eyes bursting out from under his forehead. The king said: "Get up and come with us. . . ."

But the eldest courtier croaked like a wounded animal: "I can't—I can't, Your Majesty, the king!"

The king ordered one of his courtiers: "Go fetch the rabbi. Maybe he can help."

He ran to the rabbi, who was already standing on the other side of the garden, and told him what had happened to the eldest courtier.

Hearing the news, the rabbi said: "He's probably taken something from the table. He won't be able to get up as long as he doesn't return the stolen item. . . ."

The courtier ran back and related the rabbi's words. They searched the eldest courtier and found the beautiful saltshaker in his pocket. They returned it to the rabbi, and the eldest courtier at once got up and crept away—because he was ashamed in front of the king and the other courtiers.

But Gur Aryeh said to the king: "Your Majesty, the king! If the saltshaker pleases you, you can keep it for one month. But when the month is over, you must return it into my hands."

The king took the saltshaker and returned to his palace.

After a good and peaceful sleep, the king said to his courtiers: "Now I see that the rabbi is a great person and righteous man. But the eldest courtier is a bad man and a liar. From today on, I no longer want to see his face."

And so it happened. The eldest courtier no longer appeared before the king's eyes.

Meanwhile, years passed. The king grew old, but he could not forget the palace with its exquisite garden. Often he thought: "How did Gur Aryeh secure such a palace with such a garden? And how did he serve such a meal? It's a miracle that can't be grasped."

One day the king hosted guests from a distant country, and they told the following story: "Once upon a time, the king of a far-off land wanted to hold a ball for his own highly distinguished guests. When the day of the ball came, a miracle happened: the palace—with all its food, platters, and servants—disappeared before everyone's eyes. The dignitaries came to the ball, but in vain—there was no wine, no food, no servants. The palace was dead. Three days later, the palace with all its servants and wines returned. Everything was back in its place, but one thing was missing: a valuable and beautiful saltshaker. But do you know how it happened? It had something to do with a great and righteous person. . . ."

Having heard these words, the king thought hard. For three days, he didn't speak, and on the fourth day he summoned the rabbi.

He wanted to ask the rabbi about the miraculous palace with its garden, which was so suddenly unveiled before his eyes—but he did not dare ask. It seemed to him that he mustn't speak of it, that it was a great secret, about which only a good and beautiful heart could receive an answer.

And he said to the rabbi: "My entire life, I have prepared myself to ask you something—but I feel I must not do it, because I'm not good enough and because I've spilled much blood in my wars. But there's one thing I want to ask of you. Be my friend. . . ."

The rabbi lifted two pure and good eyes and said: "I hear what you say."

And the king added: "You're a righteous man, a pure and godly person. You will be my best friend."

And so it happened. Until the king's very death, Gur Aryeh was his best friend and dearest advisor.

Translated by Sandra Chiritescu

A TREASURE IN THE SNOW

Jacob Reisfeder

There was once a teacher named Haim-Ber, who taught little children. He was a very pious, God-fearing man, but he was very poor, a pauper. His wife and eight children were almost always hungry, and in winter they froze. But his wife was good and pious. She never caused her poor, wretched husband sorrow, and she did whatever she could to provide for the children so there would be no quarrels in the house and no one would know of their poverty.

But once—in the middle of a terrible winter—for the third day in a row, there was no bread to eat and no embers in the fire. Outside there was a bitterly singeing white frost. With the entire town covered in mountains of snow. The marketplace looked as if it had been abandoned. Not a single sled had appeared the whole day. Only the wind raged, wildly tearing at doors and window shutters.

None of the townspeople, not even the stallkeepers, could be found outside. Because of the frost, the town's children had not gone to school for a number of days, and Haim-Ber had not received the few coins he normally got each week for his instruction. The heads of the households had not paid up, and so there was not a single kopeck to buy bread, and no firewood to warm up the cold, damp house. Every day, the frost got stronger. Inside their icy home, the starving children clung to one another, blew on their frozen fingers, and stared with fear at the frozen-shut white windowpanes and the thin walls, from which water trickled all over the floor. They had no strength left.

First thing in the morning, the father—stooped over in his coat—ran off to the study house, in order not to see the hungry eyes of his starving children or the look in his wife's pious eyes, which pleaded with him tearfully:

"Haim-Ber, how can you sit there with your arms crossed and watch your children go out like a light? What kind of father are you? May God not punish me for my words! Run, borrow something, leave no stone unturned, and bring something for the children!"

But Haim-Ber no longer had anyone from whom he could borrow. So he sat in a corner of the study hall and recited psalms, his lips dried out. His voice grew increasingly weaker, chocked up with grief for his wife and children. They were dying of hunger and cold at home, and there was nothing he could do to help.

While he sat in the study hall and endlessly recited psalms, his wife stood by the window, looked with swollen eyes through the frozen windowpanes, and cursed her husband in her heart. She could no longer bear to look at her poor children who were lying on the bed and, pointing silently at their mouths with trembling hands, begging her to give them something to eat.

"Murderer! Heartless man! He should have stones, not children!" Their mother ran around the house, her eyes burning. "I'll go straight to him in the study hall and ask everyone there: Does it have to be this way?"

She flung her tattered shawl on her head, ran to the doorstep, and stopped. It would be a terrible sin, she thought, if she shamed him in front of all the men in the study hall. She could forfeit her place in the World to Come.

"What, then, can I do? The children are slipping away!"

Just then, she thought of something, which made her face flare up, and yet without a moment's hesitation, she ran out of the house.

Ten minutes later, she returned, her face burning

with shame, carrying a bit of flour in a pouch hidden under her shawl.

In no time at all, she kneaded the dough, rolled it into sheets, and cut it up into little dumplings. But just then, she remembered she had no kindling with which to cook those few ungreased dumplings. Once again, her chest tightened.

What could she do now? To whom could she turn, humiliating herself, to borrow a few bits of wood? No, it would be better to perish with the children than to appear contemptible in the eyes of her neighbors.

But she looked at the bed, where the children, half-starved, lay at death's door. She grabbed a wisp of straw from the mattress and lit the oven.

The damp shredded straw burned poorly, and the pot of water was barely heating up.

She stood surrounded by smoke, coughing, her heart aching, and blew on the fire with all her strength, over and over. She burned half the straw in the mattress, but the water would not boil.

Meanwhile, night had fallen. She kindled the kitchen lamp and continued to slave over the oven. The door opened quietly, and Haim-Ber, covered with snow, stealthily slipped inside. Then he got scared and wanted to dash back out of the house. He thought that he would find Haya-Bashe asleep, exhausted from hunger, and would also curl up in his bed. In the end, she was awake, and he came home without a kopeck, just as he had left that morning. But he heard his Haya-Bashe speak to him with compassion.

"Oh well, what can you do if God does not will it? Come, sit down. I've humiliated myself to borrow a bit of flour, but there is no wood. I've been trying to boil some water with straw, but it won't boil. Ah, I can't stand on my feet anymore, and the smoke is eating through my throat and lungs!"

Haim-Ber said to her with tears in his eyes:

"Go, Haya-Bashe, lie down on the bed a little. I'll make sure the fire burns and the water boils."

She didn't want to burden him with work that wasn't his, but she had no choice. She reclined onto the bed and at once fell asleep, exhausted. Haim-Ber stood stooped over the oven, adding straw all the time and blowing into the smoke with all his strength. Suddenly the pot of water began to boil! His face beamed. He wanted to wake her up, but decided he would cook the dumplings himself and then wake her up. She would be so pleased with him, and he wanted so much to make her happy. He cooked the food and was about to go, full of joy, to wake her up, when suddenly he heard someone very old coughing hoarsely on the other side of the door, groping around for the handle in the dark. Frightened, he said:

"Who could it be, so late at night?"

He heard an old man's trembling voice, begging to be let in.

"Have mercy on an old man—open the door! I haven't eaten in three days, and I've traveled a long way. In the dark, I felt a *mezuzah*. Open, dear sir. I'm dying of hunger and cold."

Haim-Ber's heart gave a jerk. He opened the door, and in stepped a bent-over, gray-haired old man, leaning on a cane. The visitor was chilled to the bone, with pieces of ice around his beard and mustache. He was shivering from the cold.

Haim-Ber quickly offered him a stool and, without thinking for a moment, poured him a bowl of hot food. The old man made a blessing and began eating heartily. Haim-Ber stood next to him, and his heart swelled with pride that God had given him an opportunity to fortify a hungry old man.

The old man finished the bowl of food, and Haim-Ber saw that he had still not been restored. The old man's hands and feet were still trembling. It was obvious that he was still hungry.

Haim-Ber forgot about his wife and children, who had

fallen asleep starving, and poured him another bowl of food. The old man was delighted. His eyes lit up. He was a human being again. And Haim-Ber swelled with pride.

The old man finished his meal, made the blessing after food, got up, looked around the house, and said to Haim-Ber:

"Well done! You've saved my life. I would have also liked to spend the night here as well. But I see that you too need your strength restored. Such a cramped house. Well, I'll go find somewhere else to stay. Good night!"

He piously kissed the *mezuzah* and slowly walked out.

That very minute, Haya-Bashe woke up. With a weak voice, she asked her husband whether the water had boiled yet.

When Haim-Ber, confused and frightened, told her he had cooked the food himself, a big smile spread across her face. But when she stood up and peered into the pot, everything went black before her eyes. Nothing was left but a few bits of food at the bottom. Her husband, the glutton and guzzler, had eaten almost all the food himself.

She fell upon him with a cry and a shriek:

"How could anyone with a heart eat all the food and leave nothing for his poor children?"

Her anger grew, and she cursed him. She wanted to

tear him limb from limb! Haim-Ber was afraid to tell her the truth in case it made things worse. He slid over to the door and dashed out of the house.

He ran, pale and flustered, over the deep snow. And once in a while, he looked back to make sure his wife was not chasing after him.

He saw she hadn't followed him. He stood for a while in the marketplace, out of breath and with no strength left, and looked around at the dark houses. Shivering from the cold, he thought:

"I won't be showing up back at home again today. Where else can I stay the night? In the study house? The beadle might not allow it. . . ."

As he stood there and thought, he heard a familiar voice nearby crying out:

"Dear sir, dear sir, you who saved my life! Oh, help me out of the snow!"

He looked—it was the same bent-over old man to whom he'd given a bite to eat, and who now stood buried in the snow and unable to get out.

Haim-Ber ran to the spot, snow up to his belt, and tried with all his might to help the old man get himself out of the snow.

The old man lifted one foot out of the snow, but couldn't pull out the other one. He had gotten himself caught on something. With great difficulty, the old man pulled his foot out together with the object. Something heavy and black . . .

"What is it?"

Haim-Ber looked down. It was a big heavy leather pouch.

He thought that if it contained money, the pouch would belong to both of them.

But he waited.

The old man said:

"Open it already! Let's see what's inside."

Haim-Ber's hands were shaking. He opened the pouch, and his eyes were dazzled. The pouch was full of gold coins!

The old man said to him, his eyes joyful and clear:

"You will, upon my word, find a use for these coins. You have a wife and eight children, may they live long. Take it all. I give my share over to you!"

As soon as he had said these words, the old man disappeared.

Haim-Ber understood who the old man was—the prophet Elijah. He grabbed the pouch of gold coins and ran home, filled with joy. His eyes sparkling, he cried out to Haya-Bashe and the children:

"Praised be His name! He has taken pity on us. Get up—we've been saved!"

And he poured a heap of gold coins onto the table, poured and poured, and his wife and children stood with their mouths agape.

Later, when the entire town had long fallen into deep sleep, Haim-Ber's house was still brightly lit. Haim-Ber, his wife, and their children—revived and stomachs full—embraced one another in a circle, and sang and danced for joy late into the night.

Translated by Gavin Beinart-Smollan and David Stromberg

THE ENCHANTED CASTLE

Rachel Shabad

In a small, quiet town, there once lived a poor man who had three sons. Even though they were poor, they lived quietly and well. No cursing was ever heard in their home, no disparaging words ever spoken. In this way, they lived year in and year out, summer and winter, spring and fall.

Time, however, does not stand still. The man and his wife grew older, and their three sons grew to be tall and handsome, like oak trees. They felt cramped in their small home and were eager to travel the world, to see how Jews and other people lived.

They came home one day and said: "Father, we are now grown men, and our small home is too cramped for us. We would like to travel the world and see how people live. You know we are honest and enjoy work. When we earn a great deal of money, we'll return and build a large, spacious house in which we'll all live together again."

Their father listened to them and said: "Fine, children. A man must see the world and its people. But all three of you can't leave, since we're old and weak and can't be left alone. First my eldest, Shloyme, shall leave. And upon his return, my second-born, Yoysef, shall leave. Afterward Moyshele, my third-born, shall leave. But remember, children, that you must be honest and good, and God will help you."

Having listened to his father's words, Shloyme prepared to leave. He didn't have many things to take with him, and on the third day he kissed his parents and brothers goodbye. He looked one last time at their home, the place where he had been raised, and set off.

He left the town, and in front of his eyes green fields of wheat stretched outward, with a lovely little path in their midst. He set out on the path and walked and walked until it led him into a thick, quiet forest. The farther he went into the forest, the darker and quieter it became. Only the wind moved the branches, and sometimes a bird would suddenly flap its wings. . . .

Shloyme grew uneasy, and took cover under a tree.

Under another tall tree, he saw a clear spring

glistening, as if someone had tossed liquid silver onto the ground. He got up, came up to the spring and wanted to drink his fill—he was thirsty—when suddenly he saw an old man with a white beard down to his feet. His eyes twinkled with a kind, bright light. The old man called out: "You want to drink, but I want to eat. Maybe you can give me something to eat?"

Shloyme took from his bag the only challah his mother had baked for his journey and said: "Here, old man, eat in good health. I can't give you anything more or better. I don't have anything." The old man ate some challah and asked: "Where are you going and what is your name?"

"I don't know myself where I'm headed," Shloyme answered. "My path is not yet determined, but I'm going onward."

The old man was silent for a moment and then said: "In that case, maybe you would like to come with me? I will give you work and you will earn something."

Shloyme looked the old man over. A warm light emerged from his face and eyes and drew Shloyme closer. "I'll go," he said. "I'll go with you."

And together they walked through the dark forest. Shloyme noticed that the old man's feet did not touch the ground—the dry twigs and leaves did not crackle under him. Shloyme was amazed but kept silent.

Soon they reached a tall mountain on which stood a very beautiful castle. Three thick walls wrapped around the castle, with a golden door at the center.

When Shloyme approached the door with the old man, it opened on its own, and they entered the castle. For a while, Shloyme stood still in amazement: he saw gold and silver and diamonds and flowers and people in the most astonishing and beautiful clothes—but they were all turned to stone. Even the horses in their stalls, even the flowers on the windowsills, were made of stone.

The old man said: "You will live here, my child, and your job will be to walk every day through every room—through every corner and passageway of the castle—every day, and you will call out: *'Good is the person who treats others well, who is brave and courageous!'* "

And the old man disappeared.

The next day, Shloyme began his job. He walked through every room, every corner and hall, and called out in a loud voice: "Good is the person who treats others well, who is brave and courageous!"

And every time, someone answered: "Amen!"

At first, Shloyme was startled. He just could not see

the person who was answering "Amen!" And it seemed to him as if someone were floating above his head. But he overcame his fear and did his job. This way, he passed an entire day.

In his bundle, he still had a piece of challah, which the old man had left for him. He ate the challah and went to bed.

The next morning, he rose before the sun. He washed himself, combed his hair, and began to walk through the rooms. He did his job and called out: "Good is the person who treats others well, who is brave and courageous!"

And every time, someone answered: "Amen!"

When he finished his work, the old man appeared with a small package. "I've brought you some food," he said. "You must be hungry." He handed Shloyme the package.

"Are you happy with your job?" the old man asked.

"I am," Shloyme answered, and smiled quietly.

The old man disappeared again, and Shloyme sat down to eat. In the package, he found only grapes, apples, and nuts, but they tasted of every dish imaginable in the world. If you wanted to taste meat, you tasted meat. If you wanted to taste fish, you tasted fish.

In this way, an entire year passed. Shloyme became so accustomed to the castle, with its quiet rooms set in stone, that he completely forgot about the whole world.

True, he'd sometimes feel forlorn and sad: he never saw any people there. But when he called out "Good is the person . . . ," it rang in his ears the entire day, like a tender song, which would always comfort his heart.

After a year had gone by, the old man appeared and said: "Well, you can leave now. You've done your duty. I'll give you a small package that will grow in your hand every hour, and when you arrive at home, you'll be a rich man."

The old man handed him the package, and Shloyme kissed him goodbye. Then the old man placed his hands on Shloyme's head and blessed him. Shloyme set out with light and joyful steps.

On the way, his package grew from hour to hour, and when he arrived home, it was already a large pack. When Shloyme opened it, thousands of golden ducats shone inside. . . .

His father, mother, and brothers embraced him and cried with joy. They passed the day like a holiday.

The next morning, Shloyme was already talking with workers about building a large house. At the same time, Yoysef, the second-born, said: "Well, Father, now the time has come for me to see the world and earn a living."

His father said: "True, my son. Go. But remember that one must be honest and good."

Yoysef kissed his father, mother, and brothers

goodbye, and set out on the same path as Shloyme. And the same thing happened to him as to Shloyme. He also lived in the enchanted castle, but longer than Shloyme. For a full two years, he called out in every room, hallway, and corner: "Good is the person who treats others well, who is brave and courageous!"

After two years, Yoysef returned home. He didn't bring back any money, but he did bring rays of light. Wherever he went and wherever he stood, it became as bright as if the sun were following him. Soon he came to be known across the world as a great sage, and from everywhere people traveled to him for words of advice and consolation. There was no one in need whom he didn't help or whose heart he didn't brighten.

After Yoysef's return, Moyshele, the youngest, said: "Dear father, now my time has come. Let me see the world, too."

His father blessed him and said the same thing he told the others: "Be honest and good."

On a beautiful day, he bade his parents and brothers farewell and set out. He walked unhurriedly on the same path as his brothers.

Deep in the forest, he, too, met the old man, who led him into the castle. And in the castle, Moyshele did the same thing as his brothers. He, too, called out in all the rooms, hallways, and corners: "Good is the person who treats others well, who is brave and courageous!"

But Moyshele's voice was different. In his voice, one could feel his good heart, which never wished to do anything bad. While his voice resounded loudly in the rooms, it felt as if everything warmed and came back to life. Even the old man once remarked: "My child, your voice is as sweet as a prayer."

Three years did Moyshele spend there, and for three years he praised the "good person" in every dead corner of the castle. But exactly on the day Moyshele was preparing to leave, a stranger entered and set the table. Afterward, he motioned with his finger for Moyshele to sit down. Moyshele obeyed.

Such delicious dishes Moyshele had never eaten. As he rose from the table, everything began to change in front of his eyes. Everything came to life. The stone birds began to sing, the trees in the garden grew leaves, dead flowers began to bloom and spread a wonderful scent. Horses neighed in their stalls, and a herd of cows could be heard mooing. At the same time, the stone people began to move, and among them Moyshele noticed an extraordinarily beautiful girl.

Soon she came over to Moyshele and said: "I was born in this castle. My father and mother lived here as lord and lady. But God punished all of us because we behaved badly toward others. I was punished for the following: One evening, I went out for a walk. I encountered an old beggar woman, who asked me for alms. But instead of giving her alms, I set my dog on her, and it bit her badly. The old woman wept bitterly and said: 'May God punish you!' I turned into stone at once. Along with me, everyone was turned to stone, and our castle became a dead place."

The girl looked at Moyshele earnestly: "But you and your brothers saved us. Every day, I heard you calling out and I wanted to answer you, but I couldn't. Ah! How I tortured myself! But I felt how the stone was gradually dissolving inside me and how my heart was slowly filling up with warm blood. And today I suddenly felt I could take a step, and I began to walk."

And in a resonant voice, she repeated what Moyshele would always proclaim in the dead and silent rooms. Then they quietly gazed at each other and she said: "I know your name. Moyshele. . . . If you want, Moyshele, I shall give you all my fortune, everything I own, because you gave me my breath and turned me from cold stone into warm blood. Everything happened on account of you!"

Moyshele lowered his gaze and blushed with shame.

"No," he said quietly, "I don't want anything. I do not need to be paid anything. I did what I did because it is the best deed in life: we must be good to one another."

Now the old man suddenly appeared and said: "Stay in the castle, my child. That's what I instruct you to do. Truly, on account of you, the castle has been revived. Don't leave this place just when you've given every-one life."

And so it happened: Moyshele remained in the castle.

To this day, a blue flame burns on the castle's roof. Those who wander through the dark forest and notice the small flame are reminded that in that place a good person once warmed and revived bad, cold people who'd been turned to stone. And those who enter the castle to warm up are received with arms spread wide open.

Translated by Sandra Chiritescu

GLOSSARY OF UNTRANSLATABLES

Glossaries usually give the meanings of specialized words that appear in a text—usually in the same language. This one does something different: it tells the story of Yiddish words that do *not* appear in any of the stories, but for which there were no perfect English translations. Words like these are usually lost in the fray as translators find solutions that work in the target language. By providing a peek into the process, this glossary rescues some of the words that would otherwise have been lost in translation.

Arbes: Appears in "Broken In." Though *arbes* refers to a type of pea, determining which variety is difficult. It comes from the German *Erbse,* meaning *pea,* usually referring to green peas. Yiddish-English dictionaries also define *arbes* as *pea.* Yet when Yiddish speakers today say *arbes,* they often refer to chickpeas seasoned with black pepper. Yiddish has another word for *chickpea*—though it does not appear in all the dictionaries—and that's *nahit,* which apparently comes from the Turkish *nohut* through the Russian *nut,* pronounced *nōōt.* (That's not to be mistaken with the English *nut,* which comes from the German *Nuss!*) The variation appears to be related to the region. It would seem that Yiddish speakers from Russian-speaking lands used *nahit* for chickpeas and *arbes* for green peas, whereas Yiddish speakers from Poland called chickpeas *arbes.* All this would be irrelevant if, in the story, the wagon bearing the child and his mother didn't pass a field of *arbes.* It is difficult to know whether they pass a field of green peas or chickpeas—especially as it appears that both were grown at some point in the region. And so because both are in the legume family, the surest way to present the scene is to refer to a field of bean stakes and leave the rest to the imagination.

Gevaldiker: Appears in "Broken In" and comes from the German word *Gewalt,* which means *violence.* In Yiddish, however, it has broader connotations and is often used to describe anything surprising. It is used as an exclamation—*Gevald!*—comparable to *Oh no!* In the story, when the boy arrives to live with his uncle, he sees a large group of children, and the narrator describes a *gevaldiker* tumult. While it is possible to say there is a violent tumult, the tone would be considerably different from the rest of the story, so instead the scene is described as *extremely loud.*

Holipitshes: Featured in "The King Who Licked Honey" and isn't in any dictionary. It describes what the sages and stargazers eat after failing to come up with a solution for getting the king's tongue out of the jar where it is stuck. A clue to what *holipitshes* might be is that *pitsh* sounds like a Yiddishization of *peach* in English. But while there are many types of peaches—yellow, white, freestone, clingstone—there is none called *holly.* Another clue to what *holipitshes* might be is that it sounds a little like *holeptses* or *holishkes,* Slavic-origin synonyms for stuffed cabbage in Yiddish. But this dish is usually meat-based, and considering the author's sensitivity to animals—recall that in the title story the animals are not slaughtered but "unzipped" for their meat—it seems unlikely that he would feature an image of the sages eating ground beef. An investigation into the history of canning in America, however, led to a potential breakthrough: in the 1920s, the California Packing Corporation sold Holly Brand Yellow Cling Peaches. It is possible that the wordplay-loving author noticed that Holly Peaches, pronounced in Yiddish as *holipitshes,* sounds a little like *holeptses* and *holishkes,* and so invented the Yiddish American mishmash that appears in the story. Since Yiddish is written in the Hebrew alphabet and the word looks like this—הָאֱלִיפִּיטשעס—it lost all connection to an American product that actually existed. Only after discovering Holly Brand Peaches, and thinking about the ingredients of dishes originating in Eastern Europe, could the sages and stargazers finally be described simply as eating *canned peaches*.

Keylim: Used in "The Little Boy with the Samovar" and comes from the Hebrew *kelim*, a word that means *vessels*. *Kelim* is also the name of a tractate in the Mishnah, the foundational work of rabbinic literature, which set down in writing what had been transmitted as the Oral Torah. The tractate goes into detail about how to keep all kinds of vessels kosher, or ritually pure. The word is used for pots, pans, utensils, dishes, cups—anything that can be used to store or eat food. In the Kabbalah, the tradition of Jewish mysticism that influenced many Yiddish thinkers, *kelim* are the vessels that hold holy emanations. In "The Little Boy with the Samovar," the king decrees that his subjects should give up all their lead, copper, and brass *keylim* (as spelled in transliterated Yiddish), so the term loses all Jewish context and refers to anything made of metal. Most Yiddish-English dictionaries translate *keylim* as *vessels*—but this story's context gives rise to using *metalware*.

Nashn: Common but comes up particularly in "The King Who Licked Honey." It comes from the German *naschen*, which means "to nibble or snack." The word made its way into English as *nosh*, a relatively standard word for snacking or having a small meal. All these meanings, however, involve images of biting down on something. Yet, in the story, when the king is assured that no one is watching, he takes out his tongue and starts to *nashn*—an image that, with the tongue's soft flesh, does not fit with a word like *snack*. And so, to give the sense of *nashn,* he instead sticks his tongue into the jar and "licks away."

Sheyn: Common but is especially prominent in "The Enchanted Castle." It comes from the German *schön* and is usually translated as *beautiful, handsome, pretty,* or *lovely.* It is found in the song *"Bay Mir Bistu Sheyn,"* or "To Me You're Beautiful," written by Jacob Jacobs and Sholom Secunda for the Yiddish musical *I Would If I Could* (1932) and recorded in English by the Andrews Sisters, making both the song and the vocal group major hits. In the story, *sheyn* is the first word of the sentence the bearded old man asks the young men to say as they walk through the castle: *"Sheyn* is the person who treats others well, who is brave and courageous." *Sheyn,* when used to describe someone's character, refers to something beyond their appearance. While the Yiddish *gut* (pronounced $g\overline{oo}t$) means *good, sheyn* does a little more—it suggests a person is good on the inside. So when we read *Good is the person who treats others well,* even though we don't translate *sheyn* literally, we still sense that such a person is beautiful inside.

Shlang: Appears in "The Paper Kite" and comes to Yiddish from the German *Schlange,* which means *snake.* The story's significance actually depends on the double meaning of the Yiddish *shlang,* which is both *kite* and *snake.* The plot hinges on the moment when the birds ask the kite what it is—and it says it is a *shlang.* The birds have never heard of a kite, so they mistake it for a snake. The misunderstanding causes them to fear the harmless paper kite. Since there's no way to create this double meaning in English, and since the story includes lively descriptions of the kite's tail, it's possible to transfer the image of a snake from the kite to its *snaky tail.* The birds think the tail is a real snake and so are fearful of the kite.

Shmuesen: Used in many of the stories. It comes from the Hebrew *shmu'ot,* the plural of *shmu'a,* which refers to something heard. The root is used in the holiest Jewish prayer—the *Shema*—which beseeches the people of Israel to *listen* to the words being said. Because Hebrew words are often pronounced differently in Yiddish, *shmu'ot* becomes *shmues*—referring to things heard. Here we arrive at the Yiddish and modern Hebrew meaning of the word: *rumors.* Yiddish takes yet another step and turns the noun *shmues* into the verb *shmuesen,* which means *to exchange rumors, to chat, to talk with each other.* In America, the Yiddish *shmuesen* underwent another transformation into the English word *schmooze,* suggesting speaking with someone in order to make a connection. In the stories, when *shmuesen* is used, the American meaning of *schmooze* is missing altogether, and someone is simply talking with another person.

Shreklekh: Appears in "The Diamond Prince" and other stories. It comes from the German *schrecklich,* which means *terrible, horrible, awful, dreadful, frightful,* or *terrifying.* Most famously in American culture, it is related to the name of William Steig's giant green ogre, Shrek. The Yiddish word *shrek* means *fear, alarm,* or *terror,* but Steig's use of it in his children's book creates another meaning. It suggests that what frightens us might not be as scary as we thought, and might even end up saving us. For the boy in "The Diamond Prince," the sound of children crying is *shreklekh*—terrible. Steig unburied the Yiddish word, gave it richer meaning, and brought it back to life for future generations as something both scary and good.

Yid: Common, appearing in both "Broken In" and "The Enchanted Castle." It means *Jew* and comes from the German *Jude,* derived from the Hebrew *yehudi.* But it is a difficult word to translate literally. Since Yiddish was spoken almost exclusively by Jews, when they referred to a *yid,* they just meant a man, and when referring to a woman they would say, *yidene.* One can say *the man* in Yiddish by merely saying *der yid.* But when *yid* was carried into other languages, it became pejorative, and the word is defined in English dictionaries as an offensive term for someone Jewish. When in "Broken In" the mother brings over a *yid* who is the teacher, it just means she brings over a man. And when in "The Enchanted Castle" we encounter a sentence like "The *yid* grew old," again it just means "The man grew old."

ACKNOWLEDGMENTS

This collection found its way to the world thanks to two people—Beverly Horowitz and Susan Schulman—who believed in the idea of bringing the imagination of early-twentieth-century Yiddish writers into today's stark reality. Their integrity made it possible to remain loyal to the women and men whose work is presented.

The stories owe their new renderings to the translators—Gavin Beinart-Smollan, Debra Caplan, Sandra Chiritescu, Ri J. Turner, and Lena Watson—who devoted much time and careful consideration to every word and punctuation mark. The collection also benefitted from the rigor of Jenny Golub, the book's copy editor, who gave her full attention to every single detail. And special thanks to Rebecca Gudelis for her help. Extra thanks are due to Eliezer Niborski, for his innate thoroughness and linguistic expertise, and to Lena Watson, who was always there when needed.

It's possible that none of these works would be accessible today without the efforts of libraries and archives across the world—including the Yiddish Book Center, the National Library of Israel, the YIVO Institute for Jewish Research, and the New York Public Library—all of which deserve the greatest appreciation and respect.

I owe special thanks to Professor Gennady Estraikh for tips on various lexical and contextual issues, and deep gratitude to Professor David Roskies for his historical insight, moral support, and ability to constantly see the larger picture.

I am especially grateful to Aleza, my wife, for being an indispensable partner and sounding board throughout the adventure of putting this collection together.

Finally, I would like to acknowledge the authors, who often wrote these stories under difficult circumstances, and who—even if they couldn't have foreseen the resurrection of their work—created tales that genuinely reflect the eternal spirit of their mother tongue.

ABOUT THE AUTHORS

LEON ELBE (1879–1928) was the pen name of Leyb Bassein. He was born in Minsk, Belarus, and served in the military in Panevėžys, then also part of the Russian Empire and today in Lithuania. He left for America around 1904 and settled in New York, where he wrote for the Yiddish press under a number of pseudonyms. His work often portrayed the lives of Jewish immigrants who left Russia during the first revolution, in 1905. He lost his wife in 1917, dedicating his 1919 collection *In a Red Light* to her memory. With Joel Entin, he coauthored the first American reader for learning Yiddish, *Yiddish Sources* (1916), and wrote children's stories, including two series published as books: *Barney the Teacher: His Lessons and War with Tricksters in the Land of Columbus* (1914) and *The Boy and the Ring* (1929). He also published a collection of stories and poems called *The Ways of Little Kids* (1921), from which the tales in this book were taken. He worked for many years in the Yiddish educational system in New York.

SONYA KANTOR (unknown–1920) was a poet, writer, and educator. Her premature death is lamented in an obituary by Israel Rubin—one of the only extant sources referencing her—where he calls her "a person with a multifaceted erudition and, what's even more important, with a pure and intuitive understanding of the new demands of modern education." She was, it seems, a deeply devoted kindergarten teacher who'd known no Yiddish before going into the field of education. In her short life, she published two stories, included in this collection, and several translations of Ernest Thompson Seton and Rudyard Kipling, both of whom wrote about animals and may have influenced her. "Even greater than her written legacy," writes Rubin in her obituary, "is the oral legacy she left behind, with tens and hundreds of songs, plays, and stories, which are dispersed among all the places where she worked—and she worked in many places all over Poland and occupied Lithuania." She grew ill and died in Białystok, during the Polish-Soviet War (1919–1921), and when Rubin heard of her death and went to search out her grave, the beadle at the cemetery said that scores of people had died in those difficult days, and that he had no idea where she'd been buried.

JACOB KREPLAK (1885–1945) was an author, editor, and journalist. He was born in Zabłudów, near Białystok, then part of the Russian Empire and now in northeastern Poland, and later served in the Imperial Russian Army's Finnish Guards' Rifle Battalion, based in Helsinki. Kreplak deserted the army and fled to Antwerp, Belgium, where he worked as a diamond cutter while becoming active in Yiddish cultural life. He started publishing stories in 1911, writing for Yiddish newspapers and journals in Poland and Belgium and authoring his first collection, *The Situation in Finland*, in 1913. At the outbreak of World War I, Kreplak left Antwerp, arriving in America in 1915. His wife, Anna, and their daughter Sulamitis arrived in 1916, and their daughter Mary was born in New York in 1917. Around this time, he began writing for children, and he later published a collection titled *Youth* (1935), with legends from different cultures and stories about both the Old World and America.

MOYSHE NADIR (1885–1943) was the pen name of Isaac Reiss (Yitzhak Rayz). He was born in 1885 in Narayev, a town in Eastern Galicia, then part of the Austro-Hungarian Empire and today in Ukraine. In 1898, at age thirteen, Nadir immigrated with his family to New York. He did not grow up among Jews and studied in an English-language school until age sixteen. He worked as an insurance agent and window dresser, among other jobs, before discovering the Yiddish press. His earliest publications, including "Dreadfully Bad Little Poems" and "Passable Prose," appeared in the *Daily Jewish Herald* in 1902. He soon became known as a humorist, satirist, and poet. His first collection of poems was *Wild Roses* (1915), and he also wrote essays, stories, and plays, publishing dozens of books, including *Children Unfettered* (1936), from which the stories in this collection were taken. He playfully created many pseudonyms before settling on Nadir, a Yiddish expression that can be roughly translated as *Take it!*

JACOB REISFEDER (1890–c. 1942) has largely been forgotten despite writing novels, stories, plays, and poems. He was born to a Hasidic family in Warsaw, had a traditional religious education until age eighteen, and started writing in 1908. He was part of the Yiddish press in Poland, including as a staff writer for the newspaper *Haynt* from 1911 to 1915. He traveled to Argentina in 1923 but later returned to Poland. In the mid 1930s, he was on the editorial board of *Unzer Express*. He was married, and eyewitness accounts suggest he took part in literary evenings in the Warsaw ghetto, where it appears his life ended.

RACHEL SHABAD (1898–1974) was better known by her married name, Regina Weinreich. Born in Vilna—then part of the Russian Empire and now in Lithuania—she was the daughter of Zemach Shabad, a doctor, communal leader, and cultural activist who created and supported educational, vocational, and political opportunities for Jews in Eastern Europe. Regina married Yiddish linguist and YIVO cofounder Max Weinreich, whom she met when they were both teachers in Vilna. Regina and Max were traveling in Denmark with their eldest son, Uriel, when World War II broke out in 1939. Max and Uriel traveled to New York, while Regina went back to Vilna for their younger son, Gabriel. In 1940, the family reunited in New York, where Max turned YIVO's American office into its world headquarters. Uriel Weinreich went on to become one of modern Yiddish's greatest linguists, lexicographers, and educators, while his brother, Gabriel, became a professor of physics at the University of Michigan. Regina Weinreich is virtually unknown as a writer, and the stories in this collection are attributed to her for the first time. They were most likely published around 1920 in Warsaw, under her Hebrew first name, Rachel, and her last name before marriage, Shabad.

ABOUT THE TRANSLATORS

GAVIN BEINART-SMOLLAN is a doctoral student in History and Judaic Studies at New York University.

DEBRA CAPLAN is an Assistant Professor of Theater at Baruch College, City University of New York.

SANDRA CHIRITESCU is a doctoral student in Yiddish Studies at Columbia University.

DAVID STROMBERG is a writer, translator, and literary scholar based in Jerusalem.

RI J. TURNER is an MA student in Yiddish at the Hebrew University of Jerusalem.

LENA WATSON is a Yiddish translator based in London.

ABOUT THE EDITOR

DAVID STROMBERG is a writer, translator, and literary scholar. His translations have appeared in the *New Yorker, Los Angeles Review of Books*, and *Asymptote*, and his fiction in *Ambit, Chicago Literati*, and the *East Bay Review*. He is the author of four collections of single-panel cartoons, including Baddies, and a crictical study, *Narrative Faith*. He lives in Jerusalem.